# FALSE IMPRESSIONS

# MARILYN TYNER

BET BOOKS/1-58314-038-7 (CANADA $6.99) U.S.$4.99

ABESQUE

BET

OOKS

# FALSE IMPRESSIONS

She opened her eyes and lifted her hands, placing them on his chest. She had intended to push him away, but realized immediately that her action had been a mistake. Her fingers itched to explore the muscles that flexed beneath her palms.

She lifted her face and any thought of pushing him away was arrested by the look in his eyes.

Ian was stunned by the sensations created from simply holding her in his arms. When he looked into her eyes, he could no longer resist the temptation he had been fighting for weeks.

He lowered his head slowly, as if giving her time to call a halt to his purpose.

Zoe had no intention of stopping him. As his mouth came down on hers, her eyes closed and her arms came up to encircle his neck.

Zoe moaned when his tongue searched the moist recesses of her mouth.

At first he was content to stroke her back through the thin fabric. But that was simply not enough, and soon his hand came up to stroke the bare, silky skin between her shoulder blades.

She shivered in response, and Ian realized they were both on the brink of entering dangerous territory.

He loosened his hold slightly and lifted his head after one last, brief kiss.

Zoe met his gaze. The desire she had recognized earlier was still burning in his eyes. Its intensity and her own repsonses warned her of the danger of her emotions.

"I guess I'd better see what's in there to fix for dinner," she murmured, standing up.

"Zoe, don't you think we should discuss what's happening?"

"Nothing's happening, Ian," she insisted. . . .

# BOOK YOUR PLACE ON OUR WEBSITE AND MAKE THE ARABESQUE ROMANCE CONNECTION!

We've created a customized website just for our very special Arabesque readers, where you can get the inside scoop on everything that's going on with Arabesque romance novels.

When you come online, you'll have the exciting opportunity to:

- View covers of upcoming books

- Learn about our future publishing schedule (listed by publication month and author)

- Find out when your favorite authors will be visiting a city near you

- Search for and order backlist books

- Check out author bios and background information

- Send e-mail to your favorite authors

- Join us in weekly chats with authors, readers and other guests

- Get writing guidelines

- AND MUCH MORE!

Visit our website at
http://www.arabesquebooks.com

# FALSE IMPRESSIONS

## MARILYN TYNER

**BET Publications, LLC**
www.msbet.com
www.arabesquebooks.com

ARABESQUE BOOKS are published by

BET Publications, LLC
c/o BET BOOKS
One BET Plaza
1900 W Place NE
Washington, D.C. 20018-1211

First Printing: October, 1999
10  9  8  7  6  5  4  3  2  1

Printed in the United States of America

# ACKNOWLEDGMENTS

Considering the fact that I am far from being a computer expert, I owe several people my thanks for letting me know that what I envisioned in this story is actually possible. The first of these is Felix Gardenhire, a member of my Eastern Star Chapter. Even greater appreciation goes to my nephew, Anthony Wootson, who gave me the idea for the booby trap and my brother, Robert Greenhowe, who helped with the explanation about the output of the computer chip.

My information about yachts, unfortunately, did not come from personal experience. I wish to thank William and Patty Major of Bristol Yacht Services for their assistance and the very helpful information they provided.

I am also grateful to Sgt. Charles Hall of the Savannah Police Department who patiently explained some of the procedures that would be involved in the situation described in this story.

To my fellow members of the Bucks County Romance Writers, thank you for your encouragement, enthusiasm, and even for your criticism.

In addition to the above, my thanks go to many friends, relatives, and acquaintances for their encouragement and moral support.

# CHAPTER ONE

"Did you say you plan to leave on Friday?" Derek asked, frowning.

"That's right," Ian replied. He was standing at the window of his office, gazing out on the city. He loved Atlanta, with its landscape of modern skyscrapers mixed with historic old buildings.

"I can have total peace and quiet on Blake's Island to work out the problems and finalize the plans."

With his attention focused elsewhere, he had not noticed the expression on his brother's face. The silence that followed this statement drew Ian's attention back to Derek. He moved away from the window now and sat down at his desk, looking closely at his younger brother who was seated in the chair across from him.

Looking at the two men, one could see a definite family resemblance. They had both inherited their grandmother's high cheekbones and long, straight nose. One of the few differences was in their complexions. The man behind the desk had his mother's deep bronze coloring, while the younger man's milk chocolate hue came from his father.

"What's on your mind, Derek?"

"Don't take this the wrong way, Ian, but is there another reason you chose this weekend to leave town?"

"This is the first chance I've had to get away and, with the near completion of my plans, the timing is perfect. What other reason could there be?"

Derek hesitated, becoming engrossed in a nonexistent piece of lint on his slacks. His relationship with his brother had always been honest and open. Of course, he had learned to be careful not to overstep the bounds that would take him from gentle brotherly prodding to outright prying.

"Derek? I'd really like your input, but if you've made plans for the weekend I suppose I could manage without you."

"That's not it. I haven't planned anything for the weekend. It just occurred to me that it might be more than a coincidence that this weekend is Sharmane's wedding."

"So that's what's bothering you," Ian replied, the reason for his brother's hesitancy becoming clear.

"Derek, believe me, Sharmane's wedding would hardly drive me out of town. It's been over between us for more than two years and it's been almost that long since I've had any feelings for her.

"The truth is, I had forgotten the wedding is this weekend. If you were planning to attend and that's the only problem, I can go on alone. One of us can check with Dan and see if he would mind picking you up and bringing you out to the island on Sunday. He and Aunt Emma have been planning a trip to Charleston to visit his brother, but I don't think a few days' delay would matter to them."

Derek shook his head. "I had no intention of going to the wedding," he assured his brother.

Ian noticed Derek still looked dubious about the timing for his departure. He looked pointedly at his brother.

"Derek," he continued patiently, "when I use the term 'any feelings,' I mean just that. I don't hate her, I'm not angry with her, and I'm certainly not in love with her. Whenever I think about that relationship now, I wonder if I was ever really in love with her.

"I'll admit that in the days right after the breakup, I was in a rage. I'm sure that comes as no surprise to you. I've never been angrier about anything else in my life. All things considered, I think I was entitled to that much. Finding one's fiancée in bed with your cousin would tend to evoke anger, to say the least."

He stood up and walked over to where his brother sat. He looked down at him, placed his hand on Derek's shoulder and smiled.

"Actually," he added, "I think I was almost as angry with myself for being such a fool as I was with the two of them. I've recovered from that, too. I'm fine, little brother. Sharmane and Cal's wedding is the last thing on my mind right now."

Derek watched his brother closely as he spoke. He could usually tell when Ian was upset, even when he tried to hide it. He saw no reason to doubt his words now.

"Good. I just had to be sure. I'd better get going," he said, rising. "I'll give Jared a call and set up a time. See you on Friday."

After his brother left, Ian thought about his question. In spite of being six years younger, Derek had never hesitated to voice his opinion when he thought it was necessary. Neither had it ever mattered if that opinion was unsolicited.

Derek's speculation had come as a surprise simply because Ian really had not given a thought to Sharmane, or her wedding, since their breakup. He recalled seeing the invitation at his mother's house two weeks earlier, but he had paid no attention to the date.

In spite of Sharmane's deceit, he had not been surprised that his mother received an invitation. He supposed it was just a matter of common courtesy, considering the fact that she was Cal's only aunt. At least they had been tactful enough not to send an invitation to him.

Although the feelings of betrayal and anger had left him long ago, he would never forget the night his engagement had ended. Derek's words had conjured up memories of that unpleasant episode.

He had paid an unexpected visit to his fiancée. He was feeling guilty for breaking their date earlier that evening because of a meeting with a client.

Armed with roses and an apology, he had let himself into her apartment with the key she had given him. There was no sign of her and, assuming she was in bed, he had gone straight to her bedroom. To say she was surprised to see him was a gross understatement, since she was in bed, as he expected . . . but with Cal. He vaguely recalled her calling his name in an effort to stop him when he dropped the bouquet and abruptly departed.

He had never spoken with Cal after that night, although Sharmane had called the next day, giving him some lame excuse for their deceit. She had barely uttered a sentence when he had hung up on her. As far as he was concerned, there was no explanation that could appease him.

He had to admit he had been a little surprised when he heard about their engagement. He had half expected that Cal was only interested in a short fling.

It had taken him a while to recover from the shock and the embarrassment at having been played for a fool. After he had calmed down and come to his senses, he was grateful that her infidelity had surfaced before their wedding. Obviously, their relationship would have eventually encountered serious problems.

He had told Derek the truth about his feelings. He had closed the book on that chapter of his life and moved on. The experience had made him a little more cautious in his relationships, but he certainly had not become a hermit. He had known too many good and honest women in his life to allow one woman's infidelity to turn him into a misogynist.

Even if he had not put Sharmane out of his mind long ago, her wedding would be the least of his concerns at the moment. His mind was focused on his latest plans. If he succeeded, it would ensure the future of his company for many years to come. He had little doubt he would succeed, only a few minor details remained to be worked out.

For Ian, though, there was more involved than the financial security he anticipated. He admitted to himself that his ego was also involved. This particular accomplishment would give him greater satisfaction than any of his other achievements.

Derek called early Thursday morning. He had taken the first step toward the completion of their plans.

"I'm meeting with Jared this morning. I told him that the three of us would meet at a later date to firm up the plans. I'll head down to Savannah afterward. I already talked to Dad, too. I knew they were due back yesterday, but I wanted to be sure I wasn't making the trip down there for nothing."

"Good, Derek. I'll see you tomorrow."

When Ian strode through the office late Thursday morning his mind was preoccupied with that conversation. He paused only when he reached his secretary's desk.

"Any messages, Karla?"

"A few," she informed him, handing him several slips of paper.

"Your mother called, too. She said it wasn't anything important. She just wanted to let you know they're back from Florida."

"Thanks."

Ian sorted through the slips of paper as he entered his private office. He shed his jacket and hung it in the closet before rolling up his shirt sleeves and settling down to work. He took care of the messages before dialing his parents' telephone number. His mother answered.

"Hi, Mom. I got your message. How was Florida?"

"Wonderful, your father will probably bend your ear for the next ten years about the marlin that got away. I think the only thing that saved the vacation for him was the fact that he beat Ben golfing."

"Did you get down to the Bahamas?"

"Of course. Your grandmother would never have let us hear the end of it if we had traveled all the way to Miami and not gone the short distance to the islands. She had a wonderful time shopping."

"I'm sure she did. Is she around?"

"She's napping. Try calling this evening. I'm sure she'll want to tell you about her great bargains."

Ian chuckled. "I may not have a chance to call this evening, but I'll see her tomorrow. Derek told you we're heading down to Blake's Island tomorrow, didn't he?"

"Yes, he called this morning. He said you're planning to be away for a while, but he didn't say how long."

"Actually, I don't really know how long I'll be there. Probably a couple of months."

"It's too bad you're going there to work. You need a vacation."

"I promise I'll take a break when I finish this project, Mom."

"Alright, dear. Drive carefully. I'll see you tomorrow."

# CHAPTER TWO

Zoe eyed the mail on her desk as she entered her office. She had to make some headway on the accounts today. In addition to that, her absentee boss expected her to keep the store operating smoothly. She should be accustomed to his unconcerned attitude by now, she had been managing his business for two years.

Fortunately, the sales staff and clerks were usually able to handle the store themselves. Of course, if a problem arose, Zoe was the person to whom they turned to resolve it.

Later that morning, Zoe was at work in her office checking invoices and billing statements. She had received a large wholesale order and was searching through the inventory list when her computer started making strange noises.

It was not the first time she had had problems with it. If her situation was not so frustrating, it might be funny. The man sold computers and the one in her office was ridiculously out of date.

She turned off the machine and went to commandeer the one in her employer's office. She looked, but could not find the information in any of the files on the hard drive. It occurred to her that he might not deem it necessary to load the list into his system since she was the one who handled the orders.

She noticed a file box on his desk and found a disk labeled INVENTORY. After slipping it into the computer, she scanned it and realized it did not contain the list she needed. In fact, the information on the disk indicated a warehouse address that was totally unknown to her.

Why would he have a second warehouse? When had he acquired it? And why was this the first she knew of its existence? She looked at the screen again. The nagging doubts that had been in the back of her mind for some time returned.

She wrote down the address, printed the list, and returned the disk to its case. She considered retrieving her own disk and running it on his computer, but wisely decided it would be best that she not spend any more time than necessary in his office. He had left less than two hours after his arrival that morning, informing her that he would not return to the store that day.

Aware of the possible implications of this new knowledge, she did not want to take the chance that his plans would change. The best solution she could devise was to take one of the new computers from the floor. If he had a problem with that, she would simply explain that she had to take whatever measures were necessary for her to continue managing his business.

She was not really afraid of losing her job. After all, he had left the entire business in her hands for so long, he probably had no idea where to begin if he had to take over.

Even while finishing her work, she could not get her discovery out of her mind. The only explanation she could imagine was that her boss was dealing in stolen goods.

For months she had suspected that there was something not quite honest about her employer. Her parents had always told her that one sign of a person's integrity was whether or not they looked you straight in the eye. Mr. Burnett seldom looked anyone in the eye.

She told herself that her parents' test was really no reason to consider a person dishonest. Neither was her discovery proof of illegal activity. However, the latter was a tangible piece of information that raised logical questions.

The irony was that if he had not been so cheap, she might never have discovered this information. The address on the disk was important, but she knew it was not enough. She would have to check the warehouse herself.

Zoe heard the answering machine click on as she unlocked her apartment door. Dropping her purse in the chair, she hurried to pick up the receiver.

"Hello."

"Hi, baby. I was afraid I'd missed you again. I left a message for you earlier. Were you working late?"

Zoe sighed inwardly. "No, Mom," she answered patiently. "I went shopping after work. What's up?"

"I called to let you know that your dad and I will be away for a while, probably several months. Dolores and Carl have been planning a cross-country trip for some time. You remember that I told you a few weeks ago that they bought a new RV. They took a short trip up to the Poconos, but they've been dying to really break it in. They mentioned it to us over a week ago and invited us to join them, but you know your father. I finally talked him into it."

"That sounds great, Mom, but does that mean you'll all be traveling together in the RV?"

"That's right. We're planning to take our time and work our way across the country. That's why we'll be gone for such a long time. The four of us sat down last night and worked out a tentative itinerary. Of course, our plans are subject to change if we decide to take a side trip after we get on the road."

"Are you sure this is a good idea, Mom? Where will you be staying? Don't you think three months in an RV with another couple might get a little nerve-racking? Even if they are your best friends."

Zoe's mother chuckled. "Those questions sound like you're trying to turn the tables on me for the times I've questioned some of your decisions. Don't worry. We took that possibility into account.

"That's why we worked out the itinerary. Some of the time we'll use camp grounds. Since we'll be stopping in a few cities along the way, we plan to stay in hotels while we're in the cities. Dolores also had some brochures for bed and breakfasts, so we'll probably spend a few nights in some of them."

"It sounds like you have it all planned, down to the last detail. When do you leave?"

"Week after next. That's the main reason I called. I'll be so busy I may not have a chance to talk to you before we leave. I didn't want you to worry if you don't hear from us. Cleo will have a copy of our itinerary, and we'll check in with her periodically."

"You're leaving that soon?"

"We decided this is the best time of year to travel. We shouldn't have to worry about snow and it's not too hot. We'll probably hit a heat wave on our way home, though.

"Which brings me to the other reason I called. We plan to return by a southern route and I thought we'd stop and see you."

"You don't really know when you'll be coming yet, do you?"

"No. I'll give you a call when we get close to that part of the trip. Are you planning to go away for a vacation? It's about time you had a vacation."

"No, Mom. I won't be on vacation. I'll be here. I just

thought that I could take a few days off while you're here, but I probably need to plan it ahead."

"Well, I'll give you as much notice as I can, but don't worry about it, baby. We won't expect you to entertain us."

"I know that, Mom. I'd just like to be free to spend as much time with you as possible."

"Well, we'll see what happens." There was a pause before her mother continued. "There is one more thing, Zoe."

"What is it?"

"I heard that a few of the school districts in the area are hiring for the fall term. I know you're not thrilled with the idea of moving back to Pennsylvania, although I don't understand it. I put a few applications in the mail to you yesterday. Will you at least consider filing them?"

"Mom, I don't really have any great aversion to moving back to Pennsylvania. It's just that I like it here. I like Savannah. I just think I should give myself more time to find a teaching job here."

"Alright, Zoe. I'm just concerned. You're an intelligent woman and I hate to see you wasting your ability, and your education."

"I know. I guess it won't hurt to file the applications. If I'm offered a job, I can make my decision then."

The two women chatted for a few more minutes. Before hanging up, her mother reminded Zoe that her older sister, Cleo, would be able to contact them in case of an emergency.

After she hung up the telephone, Zoe sighed again. Her mother would never understand her determination not to return to Pennsylvania. Both of her parents had been upset when, after graduating from college in Georgia, Zoe had chosen to remain there and look for work.

She understood her mother's concern over her current job situation. She was not pleased with it herself. Until two years earlier, she had been a teacher in a public school in

Savannah. Then the cutbacks started. As one of the newer teachers, it had come as no surprise when she was furloughed.

Her family had urged her to return home. She had refused, insisting that she would manage. In the end, she had promised that she would give herself six months to find employment. If nothing turned up in that time, she would give serious thought to returning to Pennsylvania.

She had put in numerous applications and sent out dozens of résumés, all to no avail. Finally, she had been forced to set aside her hopes for another teaching job, temporarily. She applied for and was offered the job with Mr. Burnett, managing his electronics store and wholesale distributorship. The pay was not great, but it was sufficient to keep her head above water.

Her employer was tolerable, mostly because he was seldom around. She had recently acknowledged, inwardly, that she had allowed herself to remain in a rut, partly because his absence afforded her a great deal of freedom. The time had not been a total waste, she had earned her Master's Degree. Having done that and after admitting she was in a rut, she made a promise to herself to redouble her efforts at finding a better job.

The job itself was boring. That is, until her recent discovery. Before she started looking for another job, she had to follow through with her suspicions.

If what she suspected was true, it was no wonder Mr. Burnett had left the retail store and wholesale distributions completely in her hands. No doubt his other activities were much more profitable. It occurred to her that it was very possible he kept the legitimate business only as a cover.

Tomorrow she hoped to have an opportunity to find out what was in that secret warehouse. Mr. Burnett had already informed her that he did not expect to be in all day. That had come as no surprise. Although she would have to go in to work as usual, she was hopeful that she would be able to leave early. However, since the manage-

ment of the store usually fell entirely on her shoulders,
that possibility was slim.

Zoe was having second thoughts about her plans when
she entered the store the following morning. As the day
progressed, however, her determination returned. The
possibility of danger never crossed her mind. After all, she
was only planning to check out the warehouse and inform
the police. Chances were that it was all for nothing, anyway.
There might be a perfectly good explanation. The list she
had seen might be old and the warehouse might be empty
now.

The day seemed to drag even more than usual. Her
thoughts vacillated between curiosity and apprehension;
curiosity won. By the time she closed the store at six o'clock,
she was more than prepared to follow through with her
plans and put an end to her speculations. She had almost
convinced herself that her vivid imagination was just working overtime, but she had to satisfy her curiosity.

Zoe reached the area near the address in question and
drove around for a while looking for the warehouse. After
getting lost twice, she almost turned back. She pulled out
the map instead, unwilling to give up without having her
curiosity satisfied.

She finally found the address and circled the block,
looking for a suitable place to leave her car. Even though
the area looked somewhat deserted, it was possible that a
strange car might raise some questions, especially if the
building was occupied. She found an empty lot around
the corner from the address on the disk and parked her
car.

She got out of the car and looked around. The area was
mostly warehouses, some empty and deserted. She took a
deep breath, shouldered her purse, and started toward the

address on the piece of paper. Although she had memorized it, she wanted to be sure. It would never do to send the police to the wrong warehouse. She could imagine trying to explain that.

As she approached the building, it occurred to her that she might not be able to get in. The large double doors were padlocked, but she walked around the building until she found a side door that looked promising. She was a little surprised when it opened easily. She entered slowly, listening for any sign that would indicate it was occupied.

One of the possibilities that she had been considering was immediately discarded. It was definitely not empty. She pulled the regular inventory list from her purse and began checking it against the cartons of merchandise stacked in rows. None of the numbers on the boxes corresponded with those on her list. So much for the idea that her employer had recently purchased another warehouse, moved the regular merchandise, and neglected to inform her of the change. Considering his general disinterest in the operation of the store, that would not have surprised her.

Even when she had originally considered it, she had known that possibility was far-fetched. For one thing, it did not explain the unfamiliar inventory list. The usual merchandise included computers and their peripherals and software, as well as televisions and similar items. The strange list she found included a multitude of items.

It was this last piece of information that forced her to admit that she was grasping at straws to find a reasonable explanation for the existence of this warehouse. She did not really want to have her suspicions confirmed. She did not want to learn that she had been employed by a thief for two years.

She continued looking around, examining the numbers and names on the cartons. Finally, she decided she had seen enough to satisfy her own curiosity and to warrant reporting what she had seen and her suspicions to the police. The rest would be up to them. They would decide whether the information she had was sufficient to justify any further investigation.

# CHAPTER THREE

Zoe had turned to leave when she heard muffled voices. Following the sound, she discovered an office near the back of the building. She could just make out the forms of two men behind a glass window that looked as though it had seen no soap since the warehouse was built.

Her curiosity increased and she moved closer. The voices became more distinct and she recognized one of the men as Mr. Burnett. She could barely distinguish their words, picking up only a phrase here and there, but she understood enough of the conversation to have her suspicions confirmed without a doubt. Mr. Burnett was making plans to buy stolen software.

From what she had determined from snatches of the exchange between the two men, it seemed the other man was the thief and her boss was acting as a go-between for the buyer. Surrounded by stacks of merchandise of questionable origin, she could easily imagine him in that role.

She was so engrossed in trying to hear specific information that she realized too late that the door to the cubicle had opened. She had a glimpse of the stranger as he emerged.

Unfortunately, he and her employer also saw her, just before she turned and ran toward the exit. She heard her employer shouting at the other man to stop her and made the mistake of looking back over her shoulder and crashed into a stack of cartons. She barely managed to keep her balance.

The jolt of the collision was enough to dislodge her purse from her shoulder. It crashed to the floor, the contents scattering all around her. Her car keys skittered across the concrete, too far away for her to reach them, and she did not dare go back to retrieve them.

Zoe hesitated for only a second, hearing the footsteps coming closer. She lost her way through the stacks of cartons and had no idea in what direction to turn to find the door she had entered much too long ago. She breathed a sigh of relief when she finally saw a door. It made no difference that it was not the door she had entered earlier. At this point, any door would do. She darted toward it, pulled it open, and came to an abrupt stop.

It was now dusk—not a time of day that she had expected to be in this area of town. In that split second, she became aware that she had exited on a different side of the building from where she had entered. The street facing her was not familiar. She heard a sound behind her and bolted through the door. She ran to the corner of the building, hoping she would see a familiar sight. As she ran, her apprehension began to dissipate.

It occurred to her that the fading light would serve to make her less visible. If she could hide somewhere, her pursuer might tire of looking. Once he had abandoned the likelihood of finding her, she could worry about getting home.

If both men left the warehouse, she might even be able to sneak back in and get her keys and the other contents of her purse. If she could not manage that, there was a spare set of keys she kept in a magnetic case under the fender of her car. In any event, once she was in the clear she could worry about finding her way back to the street where she had parked her car.

When she turned the corner, she was facing the waterfront. She heard a door slam and looked around quickly for a hiding place. There were a number of large oil drums near the dock, a short distance away. Seeing no other possibility for avoiding exposure, she started in that direction. Once again, she heard faint footsteps behind her and picked up her pace.

She slipped once on the cobblestones and regretted her shortsightedness for not thinking to wear flat shoes. Of course, it had never occurred to her that she would have to make a quick getaway. It had never even occurred to her that the warehouse would be occupied or that she would be seen.

When she almost fell a second time, she quickly slipped her shoes off and continued running. Her stocking feet were only a little better than the high heels. They were not very good for traction, but at least she would not have to be concerned with the possibility of breaking an ankle.

She reached the group of oil drums and quickly slipped behind them. Looking out from the safety of her hiding place, she saw the stranger emerge from the side of the building. She had no way of knowing that knocking over the cartons in the warehouse had worked to her advantage, delaying her pursuer by blocking his path and preventing him from seeing the direction she had taken.

He slowed his pace, looking around. Then he ran over to the other side of the building and tried the door, but it was locked. She watched him carefully, as he looked around again. When he began scanning the area, searching, she became concerned. He would not have to be a genius to guess that she had managed to disappear so quickly because she was hiding. Once he guessed that much, the possibilities for hiding places would be obvious.

She began looking around for alternatives. A short distance away she noticed a marina. Zoe was not a water lover and the idea of boarding a boat was not appealing, even if it was tied up to the pier.

Not only that, it would take her farther away from her real objective. She was very quickly running out of options, however. She needed to find a place to wait out her pursuer, then she could find her way back after he and her boss left the area.

Picking her way through the oil drums, she edged slowly toward the pier leading to the boats moored there. Glancing back toward the warehouse, she could see her pursuer. He had been joined by Mr. Burnett. Evidently, the stranger was not as astute as her boss, who was now pointing to the group of oil drums.

When Zoe reached the pier she noticed a man in the booth a short distance away. She thought about simply walking up to him and explaining the situation, but when she tried to formulate such an explanation in her mind, it sounded incredible, even to her.

If the guard did not believe her, he would refuse to allow her access and she would have exposed herself to her pursuers. She was trying to solve the problem of getting around him when he left the booth and walked toward one of the boats.

Taking immediate advantage of his absence, she hurried down the planked walkway, shoes in hand. He was just a short distance ahead of her, giving her no time to pick and choose a boat for her hiding place. The first boat that looked deserted would have to suffice. There was a yacht close at hand, easily accessible from the pier. There were no lights on and she hurried aboard.

Crouching down in the shadows behind the partition on the bridge, she could see no sign of the stranger at first. A moment later, she had a glimpse of him searching through the oil drums she had wisely abandoned. Her attention was drawn from him when she heard voices on the pier, just outside the yacht. She shrank deeper into the shadows.

"I was wondering where you were, Joe."

"I thought I saw a light at one of the other boats that's supposed to be vacant. Is anything wrong?"

"No, I guess not. Good night."

The voices were not familiar. The conversation in the warehouse had been muffled, but she would not forget the voices. Neither of the men on the pier was the one who had been chasing her.

Unfortunately, this new stranger posed a different threat. He was preparing to come aboard. If he found her, he would probably assume she was a burglar. The explanation she had tried to formulate for the guard at the booth sounded no more credible as a reason for her being on his boat.

She quickly ran down the stairs from the bridge and found herself in the salon. She moved away from the steps just in time. The stranger descended them, too, just seconds behind her.

She hurried down a second set of stairs, opened the door and realized she was in a hall. Wary that he might also continue down this second set of stairs, she quickly looked for a place to hide. Reasoning that the doors off the carpeted hallway must lead to sleeping cabins, she opened the first door. It was not a cabin as she had hoped, but the bathroom, or whatever it was called on a boat.

The footsteps were softer now, but they were just outside the door. She shrank away from the sound of soft footfalls and backed into the door of the shower stall. Without thinking, she entered the stall quickly. By now, she was beginning to panic. There was nowhere else to go. If he opened the door to the room, he was bound to see her shadow behind the shower door. If that happened, there was no way she could avoid being discovered. She held her breath.

Seconds later, she heard footsteps above her and

another man's voice call down the stairs. The man in the hall answered and, a moment later, she heard his footsteps retreating. She came out of the shower stall slowly, listening to make sure the voices were still coming from the bridge.

She had to get off the boat. How had she managed to get this far off track? It was supposed to have been a simple matter of checking out the warehouse and, if necessary, notifying the police.

She remembered that there had been large windows in the salon. The voices were still directly above her. If they remained on the bridge for a while, maybe she could climb out a window and get off the boat.

Cautiously, she poked her head out the door and listened a moment. She crept to the foot of the stairs, listening through the door to be sure there was no one on the other side of it. She could hear the voices more clearly, although she could not decipher the words. The gist of the conversation became clear just as she opened the door and the boat lurched. Zoe was taken by surprise and as it began to move, she was thrown off balance and she fell, hitting her head on the doorjamb.

Up on deck, Derek returned from loosing the moorings and took a seat on the bridge next to his brother. Ian manuevered the yacht from the slip and headed out into the bay.

"You checked everything when you came aboard?" Ian asked as he steered the boat. "How long had Joe been away from the booth?"

"He couldn't have been gone long. I noticed him the first time I drove past the pier. After I parked and reached the booth at the pier, he was gone. I'd say he wasn't away from the booth more than a few minutes. And, yes, I gave the *Queen Bea* a once-over."

Ian nodded and they proceeded to the island.

* * *

The *Queen Bea* slowly approached the dock jutting out from the island. Ian shut down the motor while Derek handled the ropes mooring the vessel to the pier. It was fully dark now and the pier was lit by two lampposts, one on either side. About a hundred yards from the pier, past the beach, they could see the lights of the house.

Derek returned and informed Ian, "I saw Aunt Emma and Dan yesterday. They had stopped to visit Mom and Dad before going to Charleston. Dan mentioned that he had talked to you. He said they plan to be away for a few months. Since they're not going anywhere special, he said to tell you to let them know if you need them to return to the island sooner than that.

"I've been trying to convince them to go ahead and take their trip. He said he didn't feel comfortable leaving the island deserted for that long." He smiled and added, "Aunt Emma was a little put out with both you and Dan. She insisted that she's paid to keep house when it's occupied, not just to take care of it when it's empty. She also told me to tell you that she had prepared a few meals and put them in the freezer. She wanted to be sure you eat properly, since you'll be so busy."

Ian looked searchingly at his brother. "Was Aunt Emma really upset? She didn't think I was putting her out, did she? Or was it just part of her usual complaining when we refuse to let her run our lives."

Derek laughed. "Just the usual complaining. She just didn't expect that you'd be here while they're gone. In fact, I think she doubts that you will be here alone. I think she has it in her mind that you're really bringing a woman with you and you didn't want her nosing around."

Ian shook his head. "What about Dan? I only spoke to him on the phone, but he didn't give any indication that there was a problem, or that this wasn't a good time."

"No problem. He said his brother and sister-in-law have

been after them for a while to come for a visit. For them, the timing didn't make much difference."

"Good," Ian said, reaching for the bag he had brought aboard. "Well, everything's settled here for the night. Let's go."

"I just need to get some things from below," Derek said, starting down the stairs.

A few minutes later, he called up to Ian. "You'd better come down here."

When Ian reached the stairs, the door was propped open and Derek was kneeling beside Zoe. A myriad of emotions raced through Ian.

"Is she alright?" he asked, making his way down the stairs.

"I think so. It looks like she bumped her head, either on the stairs or the doorjamb."

"Who is she? What's she doing here? I thought you said you checked the *Queen Bea?*"

"Chill, Ian. I did check. She must have been hiding in a closet or something. As for who she is, I have no idea. Does she look familiar to you?"

Ian was kneeling on the other side of her now. "Never saw her before in my life."

Placing an arm beneath her, he suggested, "We might as well take her up to the house."

He lifted her limp body and hesitated a moment before starting back up the stairs. Derek retrieved both of their bags and followed him.

# CHAPTER FOUR

Derek caught up with Ian as he reached the path to the house. He ran ahead, unlocking the door and holding it open for Ian, who carried his burden into the living room.

After laying her on the sofa, he hesitated a moment, taking in her physical appearance. Her beige linen suit and the high heels that had been found on the floor beside her did not conform with the usual image of a burglar. He sat down beside her on the edge of the sofa. His gaze wandered over her smooth brown skin, long lashes, and finally settled on her full lips.

He remembered their assumption that she had hit her head on the stairs. He raised his hand and gently ran his fingers through her short, silky black curls.

When his fingers touched a lump at the back of her head, she stirred for the first time since he had lifted her into his arms. Her eyelids fluttered open and Ian felt a strange stirring as he stared into eyes the color of milk chocolate.

"Who are you?" she murmured, wincing from the pain when she tried to sit up.

Her question broke the spell that had held him in its grasp since the moment he touched her. He took a pillow from the other end of the sofa and eased it behind her. His thoughtful action was automatic. It was no indication that his suspicions had diminished.

"Considering the fact that you stowed away on my yacht, I think I should be asking the questions, but I'll answer yours first. I'm Ian Roberts, this is my brother, Derek."

"Your yacht? What happened?"

"Why don't you tell me. What were you doing on the *Queen Bea*?"

Zoe frowned. "I don't know."

Ian stood up. His expression hardened. "Fine. Let's start with something simple. Who are you?"

Zoe just stared at him, a puzzled expression on her face. Ian's patience was rapidly disappearing.

"Look, lady. That's not a difficult question. What's your name?"

Tears sprang up in her eyes. "I don't know," she whispered, wiping at the moisture with the back of her hand. Again she tried to sit up, but fell back against the pillows. "My head hurts. What happened?"

Before Ian could reply, Derek spoke up. "We think you must have bumped your head somehow, when you were on the yacht. It's the best explanation we could come up with. I'll get you something for your headache."

She turned her head gingerly, looking around. "This isn't a boat. Where are we?"

"We're on an island," Ian informed her. "Derek found you lying at the foot of the stairs on the yacht when we arrived. This is my house."

He folded his arms across his chest. His eyes held hers as he continued. "Do you really expect me to believe that little bump on the head caused amnesia?"

"I don't care what you believe," she said, trying to hold back the tears. "It's the truth."

"You have no recollection of boarding the *Queen Bea*?"

"I told you, I can't remember anything. Why would I lie about something like that? Don't you think I want to remember?"

As she uttered the last sentence, she could hold back the tears no longer. She lowered her head in an attempt to block out his probing gaze. In spite of the tears, Ian was not totally convinced, and his patience was wearing thin.

In the middle of his brother's interrogation, Derek returned with an ice pack and aspirin. He could see that Ian was not buying her story and he understood his brother's apprehension, but he also sympathized with her.

If she actually did have amnesia, no amount of questions or threats would give Ian the answers he sought. Her persistent denials indicated she was not faking the memory loss. He could only imagine how frightening such an experience must be. It was time for him to keep his brother's suspicions from getting out of hand.

He handed Zoe the aspirin and a glass of water. After she swallowed the pill, he gave her the ice pack. She held it to her head and closed her eyes, trying to will away the pain.

"Ian, can I see you in the kitchen?"

Ian hesitated, then sighed and followed his brother out of the room. He could guess what was on Derek's mind, but he was determined not to let his guard down. The sudden appearance of a strange woman at this crucial time was a bit too coincidental to suit him. On top of that, he was expected to accept a second coincidence of amnesia. That was just too much.

"Ian," Derek began, "I know what you're thinking, but try to lighten up. I think she's telling the truth. I can't believe what we saw in there is an act. Besides, in a few days I'll take her back to Savannah. What harm can she do between now and then?"

"Alright, Derek. I'll 'lighten up,' as you say, but she's not leaving Blake's Island until this project is completed."

Derek could not believe his ears. Ian could not be suggesting what he thought he was suggesting.

"What do you mean, 'she's not leaving the island?' "

"Just what I said. She'll stay here until the project is completed."

Derek's mouth dropped open. "Ian, are you crazy! You can't just keep her here against her will. That's the same as kidnapping."

"Calm down, Derek. She chose to stow away on my yacht. I'll take her back when it's convenient for me. Anyway, if she really has amnesia, we have no way of knowing where she lives."

"You know that's a cop-out, Ian."

"Derek, think about what's at stake here. We have no idea who she is or why she was aboard the *Queen Bea*. Maybe it is a cop-out, but I won't jeopardize everything now. She'll be fine right here. In fact, she might be better off here until her memory returns."

Derek shook his head. He had lived with his brother's stubbornness all his life. There had been a few times when he had actually been able to talk Ian into a compromise. The look on his brother's face told him he would never win this particular argument.

"Fine, Ian," he replied, turning abruptly and leaving the room.

Ian followed. They returned to the living room to find Zoe asleep. Ian stood looking at her for a moment before gently shaking her shoulder.

She stirred and opened her eyes. Thanks to the aspirin and the ice pack, the throbbing in her head had eased a little. This time when she tried to sit up, she succeeded.

Before she could enjoy the cessation of pain, however, she was faced with another problem. She closed her eyes and took a deep breath, trying to will the nausea away. It was no use.

"Where's a bathroom?" she mumbled, her words barely coherent.

The abrupt question caught Ian off guard. "A what?"

"A bathroom," she repeated, trying with all her energy not to give in to the queasiness.

The look on her face explained the urgency in her voice.

"Down the hall," he said, pointing. "The first door on the left."

In spite of the throbbing in her head, Zoe hurried down the hall in her stocking feet. Even from where the two men stood, they could hear her retching. Derek looked pointedly at Ian.

"Alright, Derek. I'll concede that the amnesia might not be faked. In which case, I have to stress my opinion that remaining here is probably the best thing for her."

"You're still rationalizing, Ian. What if she has a concussion?"

"I seriously doubt that. That little bump on the head hardly seemed sufficient to cause a concussion."

He tried to ignore the nagging voice in his head that reminded him that he had not thought it serious enough to cause amnesia, either. He had a sudden unwelcome vision of her as he had seen her a few minutes earlier, her head bent as she attempted to wipe away the tears.

Ian sighed in resignation. He loved his brother, but sometimes he thought Derek took the idea of being his brother's keeper too literally. He seemed to feel it necessary to prick Ian's conscience periodically.

"If it will make you feel better, I'll keep an eye on her tonight. Isn't it the usual procedure to wake the patient every couple of hours to make sure they're coherent?"

He walked over to his brother and put his hand on his shoulder. "I'm not as callous as I may sound, Derek. If I thought she was seriously injured, I wouldn't hesitate to take her to a hospital. And, I promise not to ask her any more questions tonight. Okay?"

Derek nodded. He had never known his brother to be

uncaring and he did not believe it now. The present situation had simply made him overly cautious.

Their attention was drawn to Zoe as she returned from
the bathroom, her hand on the wall as if she needed its
support. Ian went to her aid, taking her arm and helping
her back to the sofa. He urged her to lie down, but she
shook her head.

"I'm better now."

"I suppose after that, you wouldn't be interested in
something to eat, would you?"

"I don't think that would be a good idea."

"How about a cup of tea?"

Zoe looked at him uncertainly, taken off guard by the
change in his attitude. Derek smiled at his brother's questionable solicitude.

"A cup of tea would be fine. Thank you."

Derek sat down beside her while Ian went to get the tea
he promised. "Feeling a little better now? How's your
head?"

"It's okay. That's the least of my problems."

"I wouldn't worry about the memory thing too much.
I'm sure it will all come back to you."

"Isn't there usually another word that belongs on the
end of that sentence, such as, 'eventually?' How long is
'eventually?' "

Derek laid his hand on top of hers. "I'm sorry. I don't
know what to say. I guess it's easy for me to tell you not
to worry."

A few minutes later, Ian returned with her tea. He set
the tray on the table in front of her. She reached to pick
up the teapot and he noticed her hand trembling.

"Let me," he offered, placing his hand over hers.

Zoe was startled by the tingling sensation that traveled
up her arm. Ian poured the tea and handed her the cup.
As she sipped her drink, he excused himself. Retrieving
his bags from the entrance hall, he carried them down the

same hall where she had gone to the powder room just a few minutes earlier.

Derek followed suit, taking his bags to the hall on the other side of the living room. Zoe was left alone to contemplate her situation.

What possible reason could she have had for stowing away on his boat? More importantly, why couldn't she remember? Surely, if the bump on the head was responsible for her memory loss, she would have worse physical symptoms than the nausea and headache. The nausea had faded and the headache was now nothing but a minor throbbing. Before fear and panic had time to really take hold, Ian and Derek returned. Ian picked up her shoes from the floor beside the sofa.

"I've prepared a room for you," Ian told her, holding out his hand. "You'll feel better after a good night's sleep."

Too exhausted and confused to argue, Zoe took his hand and stood up. He led her down the hall where he had taken his bags. Opening the door to the bedroom across the hall from his own, he ushered her in.

Sensing she was still none too steady on her feet, he gestured to the chair and then walked over to the closet. Zoe took in the obviously feminine decor and began to have doubts about the arrangement. Before she could voice her concern, Ian had finished sorting through the clothes. He pulled out a gown and robe, holding them up for her inspection.

"I'm not sure about the pajamas, but these should fit."

He did not notice her expression until he was returning from the closet.

"I . . . I don't think I can sleep here. The sofa will be fine."

Ian's expression softened. He opened his mouth to speak and then hesitated, not knowing what to call her.

"You can't sleep on the sofa. You need a good night's rest."

Zoe hesitated. The throbbing in her head and the nausea had subsided, but the bed did look inviting.

"You're probably right. I guess whoever's room this is wouldn't mind my sleeping in her bed. The clothes are a different matter. I don't think your girlfriend, or whoever owns those clothes, would appreciate a stranger wearing them."

"This room happens to be the one our sister uses when she visits. The clothes belong to her and, under the circumstances, I'm sure she won't mind."

Zoe's uncertainty was written on her face. "Your sister?"

"That's right, my sister. So, will you please accept my hospitality, before you fall flat on your face?"

"I suppose I don't have any choice," she conceded.

"The bathroom is through that door. Help yourself to whatever you need."

He lightly touched her shoulder and Zoe felt that strange tingle again. "Get some sleep."

Without another word, he turned and left, closing the door behind him. Zoe stood looking at the door for a moment before turning her attention to the room.

The pale aqua walls and deep turquoise carpet were the perfect backdrop for the white wicker furniture. The queen-size bed was covered with a blue and lavender flower print bedspread. In the corner, near the sliding glass doors, sat an extra large armchair and an ottoman, upholstered in the same flower print.

She walked over to the door he had indicated and opened it. It seemed a bit understated to use the mundane term bathroom to describe the luxury that faced her. The turquoise carpet was the same as in the bedroom. Surprisingly, the fixtures were white, but certainly not what one would consider standard.

The raised whirlpool tub was enclosed in turquoise-veined marble, the same as the sink on top of the white wicker vanity base. The ledge of the tub held a collection of glass jars in blue and lavender, presumably containing various bath salts and oils.

The thought of a soothing bubble bath was tempting, but she was too unsteady to give in to it. With her luck, she'd probably fall and really end up with a concussion this time. She briefly considered the possibility that another bump on the head might restore her memory. *Well,* she thought, *at least my sense of humor is intact.*

She took a deep breath, trying very hard to push aside her fear. It would not help to allow herself to give in to her previous anxiety.

Returning to the bedroom, she stripped off her suit and blouse and hung them in the closet. She eyed several other articles of clothing hanging there and recalled Ian's statement that the pajamas might not fit her. She had to admit that his assessment was correct. She might be able to get by with some of the looser garments, but most of the clothes would never fit.

Although the clothes were not those of a model-thin woman, it was questionable whether she could squeeze her ample figure comfortably into the majority of the garments. Not that it mattered. She could wear her own clothes home the next day.

Home! Where was home? Where would she go when they took her to the mainland? There was no point in dwelling on those questions. Derek could simply take her to the police. They would help. She had to cling to that hope.

She entered the bathroom and stripped off the remainder of her clothes. After washing, she managed to find a toothbrush, still in its wrapper. Picking up the underwear she had shed, she realized that she would have no others to wear the next day. As bad as she felt, she had no choice but to wash them and hope they would dry overnight. Her ablutions completed, she donned the nightgown, turned out the lights, and crawled gratefully into bed.

* * *

Her sleep was interrupted several times during the night by Ian. When he awakened her for the third time she became angry.

"How many fingers am I holding up?"

"Fifty," she retorted. "Go away and leave me alone."

"I have to be sure you don't have a concussion."

"I don't have a concussion and you were the one who insisted that I get a good night's sleep. How do you expect me to do that when you wake me up every ten minutes."

Ian smiled. "It's only been every few hours. From your response, I think I can safely assume that you suffered no serious damage from that bump on the head. I won't disturb you again. Go back to sleep."

She was asleep again almost immediately. Ian took the opportunity to check her clothes for sizes. Since he planned to keep her on the island, she would need more clothes.

# CHAPTER FIVE

When Zoe opened her eyes the following morning, she was still disoriented. Her eyes finally focused on the unfamiliar surroundings. When she sat up, the slight throbbing in her head reminded her of the previous evening's events. Unfortunately, that was all she remembered.

She got out of bed and made her way to the bathroom in search of aspirin. After downing two pain relief tablets, she went to the tub and turned on the faucet. Sniffing the contents of a few of the jars, she settled on lavender bubble bath and oil. As the bubbles began forming, the warm water brought forth a soothing aroma that wafted up to her nostrils. A few moments later, she was lying back against a sponge pillow, luxuriating in a mountain of fragrant bubbles.

Sometime later, Zoe stood in front of the open bedroom closet, sifting through the hangers of clothes. She had no idea what time they would be leaving for the mainland and there was no point in lounging around in her suit. Fortunately, her underwear had almost dried overnight. A little help from a hairdryer had completed the process.

She finally settled on a loose-fitting dress in a geometric print of blues and greens with short sleeves and an empire waist. She was just slipping it over her head when her stomach put in its bid for attention. She had no idea when she had last eaten. She did recall that she had eaten nothing since being found aboard the boat, thanks to the nausea from her bump on the head.

When she exited the bedroom, the smell of coffee drew her to the kitchen. There was a man sitting at the table reading a magazine, an empty plate in front of him. Her mind was still a little fuzzy. She thought she remembered his name was Derek.

He looked up and smiled. "Good morning. I hope you're feeling better."

"Yes, thank you."

"I know you weren't quite yourself last night. I'm Derek."

"Yes, I remember. Where's Ian?"

"He had to go to the mainland early this morning." He looked at his watch. "I expect he'll be back very soon."

He gestured to the counter. "There's coffee already made. There's also juice in the refrigerator. What would you like to eat?"

"You don't have to wait on me. If you just show me where everything is, I can fix it myself."

"No problem," he insisted, laying the magazine aside. Walking over to the cupboard, he pulled out a mug. "Would you like some coffee?"

"Yes, please."

After setting the mug in front of her, he indicated the cream and sugar. "So, what'll you have? How about an omelet? Or scrambled eggs with bacon or sausage? We even have an assortment of cereals."

Less than ten minutes later he set a plate containing a western omelet in front of her. Derek removed his empty plate from the table and placed it in the dishwasher. Then he refilled his mug and joined her at the table while she ate.

"Where, exactly, are we? Is there a town nearby?"

Derek shook his head. "I'm afraid not. It's a private island. We're about thirty miles south of Savannah. The island's been in my family for generations."

"You own the entire island?"

Derek smiled. "It's a very small island, less than fifteen square miles in area. It's a rather interesting part of our family's history." He looked embarrassed. "I'm sorry. I guess I'm getting a little carried away."

"No, please continue. I'd like to hear about it."

"It was a grant awarded to my mother's great-grandfather, not that he ever made much use of it. At the time, it was too far from the mainland for practical access. He had no children by his wife, so he generously left it to his only son by his slave mistress. That was my grandfather. He, in turn, passed it on to his children. Only one of them had children—my mother and her brother. My uncle died about eight years ago and my cousins showed no great interest in it, so Ian bought them out a few years ago and built this house."

"Isn't it inconvenient, living out here?"

"He doesn't live here all the time. It's more of a retreat for the whole family."

Derek realized that he had been carried away reminiscing about his family and answering her questions. So far, her questions had been innocuous, but they could easily become more probing.

He wished that Ian would return. He did not want to be on the receiving end of any questions concerning her return to the mainland. He was not to be that lucky.

"When are we going back to the mainland?"

"I'll be returning to Savannah in a few days."

Something in his voice alerted Zoe. "Ian's not going with you?"

"No," Derek replied, cautiously. "He'll be staying here for a while—probably two or three months."

"So, you'll be taking me back?"

Derek hesitated just long enough. He breathed a sigh of relief when he heard the front door close. He had not escaped some of the questions, but he was grateful that the worst news would have to come from his brother.

Ian joined them in the kitchen, his arms laden with packages. "Good morning. I see Derek's fed you. You weren't very interested in food last night. How are you feeling today?" he asked, setting the bundles on an empty chair.

"Much better, thank you."

"I bought a few things for you. I'll put them in the bedroom."

"You didn't have to do that. There are a few dresses in the closet that will fit. I could have managed for a few days, especially since you insisted your sister wouldn't mind my making use of them."

Ian and Derek exchanged glances as she rose to take her empty dishes and put them in the dishwasher. She refilled her mug and returned to the table. Derek excused himself and rose to leave the room. He followed Ian to her bedroom.

"I think you'd better tell her the truth as soon as possible," he murmured as Ian deposited the packages on the bed.

"She's under the impression that I'm taking her back to Savannah when I leave."

"And, of course, you did nothing to contradict that assumption."

"That's right, big brother. I understand why you made your decision, but it was *your* decision. You can explain it to the lady."

"Actually, there's no need to explain." He shrugged. "She can't really do anything about it if I just refuse."

Derek stared at his brother a moment before turning

away in disgust. After their discussion the night before, he should not have been surprised at his brother's statement. He admitted Ian had reason to be worried, but his attitude was beginning to bother Derek.

Ian sighed in resignation when he saw the expression on his brother's face. "Derek, I know you're upset about my decision, but I have to do this my way. When it's all over, I'll explain everything. Of course, depending on who she is, explanations may not be necessary."

Derek was only slightly appeased, but he had no chance to reply before Zoe appeared in the doorway. She looked from one to the other. She had the feeling that she had missed something important. Their expressions told her that much, but neither man was forthcoming with an explanation.

Derek made a quick exit. Ian watched him go and decided that this was as good a time as any to tell her the news. He indicated the packages.

"I suppose you noticed the bathroom is stocked with toiletries. You should find anything else you need in those bags."

"I still don't understand why you went to all of this trouble. Derek said we'd be leaving in a few days."

Ian took a deep breath. "I believe what Derek said was that he will be leaving in a few days. You and I will remain here until I finish what I came to do."

Zoe could not believe what she was hearing. "But Derek said you'll be here for months. I can't stay here that long."

"As far as leaving this island is concerned, you have no choice in the matter."

"You can't keep me here against my will! That's kidnapping. What possible reason could you have for this? I'm not asking you to make a special trip. I can go back with Derek."

"I'm afraid not."

She picked up one of the bags and shoved it at him.

"You might as well take those clothes back. I don't want anything from you."

Ian shrugged. He folded his arms across his chest, refusing to take the package. "That's your decision. You can walk around in sheets if you choose." His gaze surveyed her voluptuous curves. "Or nothing at all."

He looked up from his inspection, directly into her eyes. "Furthermore, may I remind you that you stowed away on the *Queen Bea*. I did not kidnap you."

"Keeping me here against my will is the same as kidnapping," she insisted, her hands on her hips.

"Maybe. I guess we'll find out the answer to that in a few months. For now, you'll be my guest until I'm ready to leave the island.

"Besides, where would you go? Has your memory returned? Do you remember where you live?"

Tears formed in her eyes at his reminder. They were the same questions she had agonized over herself. She turned her head to avoid his gaze.

Ian felt like a snake. He was also surprised at this twinge of guilt. He took the package from her hand and tossed it onto the bed. She looked up at him when he took her hand in his.

"I'm sorry. That was a cheap shot. I can only imagine what you're feeling and that remark was uncalled for. For what it's worth, I assure you, you'll be safe here, and it will give you time to recover."

He dropped her hand and pointed to the bundles on the bed. "There's an assortment of clothes there. They should fit well enough."

He looked her up and down. "You're still welcome to supplement them with anything from the closet."

Zoe nodded. In light of his adamant refusal to consider returning her to the mainland, there was no way she could bring herself to thank him. Providing clothes for his unwilling guest was the least he could do. She turned away from him and began opening the bags.

Ian watched her for a moment. The temptation to explain further was strong, until he remembered what was at stake.

"If there's anything else you need, just let me know," he murmured.

After he left, Zoe continued to unpack the bags. She was still angry, but she realized that he had a point. Where would she go if she returned to the mainland? She could go to the police, as she had considered earlier, but what could they do? Unless someone had filed a missing persons report that fit her description, they would be of little help.

The information she had received from Derek indicated the yacht had been moored near Savannah, so she could assume she lived in that city. Beyond that, she had no idea where to start trying to piece her life together. Until she remembered her name at least, there was little chance of learning anything else about her life.

As she sorted through the clothes he had purchased, she was stunned by the assortment. There were sundresses, shorts, skirts, blouses, and two bathing suits as well as several pairs of sandals. He had overlooked nothing, including a large straw hat to protect her from the often relentless sun.

When she unpacked the lingerie, she blushed. She was even more embarrassed when she looked more closely and saw that the sizes were correct. She wondered briefly how he had obtained that particular information, but decided it was best not to explore that question any further.

After she put away the clothes, Zoe made the bed and tidied up the room. While she was tidying up she noticed a small bungalow a short distance away, behind the main house. It was strange that neither man had mentioned the presence of other people on the island. In fact, they had given her the distinct impression that it was deserted, except for the three of them.

She opened the sliding French doors and stepped out onto a deck. She walked to the railing and realized it stretched the entire length of the main house. Peering at it through the trees, she saw the bungalow appeared deserted. She wanted very much to examine it more closely. She was tempted to do just that, but decided that it was best to wait. If it was occupied, surely she would see some sign of its residents in the next few days.

Meanwhile, a long day stretched ahead of her. She decided that, aside from the bungalow, it would be a good idea to explore her surroundings. If she was going to be stuck here for two or three months, she might as well make the most of it.

There was no sign of either of the brothers as she came down the hall. When she neared the kitchen she heard voices coming from a room off the other hallway. She approached slowly, following the sound, and peeked through the open door. Ian and Derek were engrossed in conversation, poring over the papers scattered on the desk.

Ian looked up and saw her. He paused in the middle of his sentence. "Is there something you need?"

"Under the circumstances, don't you think that's a rather absurd question?" She paused, but before Ian could think of a response, she added, "I planned to go outside and have a look around. Unless you have some objection. Did you plan to keep me confined to the house?"

Ian's exasperation was evident on his face. Derek turned his head, trying to hide his amusement. This woman was obviously no scared little rabbit. His brother might have the upper in hand in the situation, but Derek had no doubt she could give Ian a run for his money if she put her mind to it.

Before he turned away, Zoe noticed the expression on Derek's face. His reaction gave her a small measure of satisfaction.

"I have no objection," Ian finally responded. "There's no reason to attempt to confine you to the house. You're free to explore wherever you choose."

Without another word, Zoe turned and walked back

down the hall. When she passed through the living room this time she paid attention to the furnishings. Until now, the decor had been the last thing on her mind.

The room was huge. To her right, just past the study was a dining area set off by several oak columns. There was an oak table that looked deceptively small for the space it occupied. She assumed there were leaves that could be added to fill an area that would easily accommodate twenty people. The oak-stained French doors on the other side of the table opened onto the same deck that was accessible from her bedroom and the kitchen.

On the other side of the hallway was the living room. Its most impressive feature was the stone fireplace that took up most of the wall perpendicular to the large windows that looked out on the ocean. Facing the fireplace was a large, overstuffed, L-shaped sofa in pale gold, arranged so that the corner of the L shape was directly in front of the fireplace. The sofa and the large square coffee table created a distinctly separate and very cozy area.

The sofa was sprinkled with half a dozen throw pillows in a pale paisley print of royal blue, green, red, and gold. The same paisley print covered the Parsons chairs in the dining area.

The expanse of gleaming hardwood floor was enhanced by beautifully patterned rugs that also separated the areas. At the other end of the room was a sofa upholstered in a striped fabric with the same rainbow of colors. It was the same sofa upon which she had been deposited the previous evening. The sofa was flanked by two armchairs in the same gold as the sofa across the room. An assortment of large floor pillows in either the gold or paisley fabric were scattered in each area. She paused a few minutes, taking in the cozy ambience, and then continued on her path toward the door.

# CHAPTER SIX

Zoe exited the front door and stopped dead in her tracks. The view was breathtaking. The wide expanse of the perfectly landscaped lawn sloped down gradually. The grassy expanse was surrounded by a stone retaining wall that separated it from the beach. A huge weeping willow stood to the right near the wall, shading a large wooden gazebo.

Off to the right past the gazebo, the lawn continued to the edge of a woods with more willow trees, live oaks, Scotch pines, and sea grass. Her attention was drawn to the pier. The yacht! There had to be a radio onboard! So, he thought she had no choice but to accept his orders.

She hurried down the stairs, across the lawn, and down the beach, looking back at the house a few times to assure herself that Ian had not decided to take one of his breaks from working. There was a cabin cruiser in addition to the yacht and an outbord motorboat. She reached the cabin cruiser first and climbed aboard. She found the radio, but after several attempts to raise a response she gave up. She moved on to the yacht.

Zoe boarded the yacht and looked around the bridge until she located the ship-to-shore telephone. She flicked the switch and spoke into the receiver. After receiving no response, she began turning various dials. Once again, she received no response to her plea. In fact, she heard no noise at all, not even static.

She was beginning to think that she must be doing something wrong. She fiddled with the knobs and dials again, to no avail. She almost jumped out of her skin when she heard a voice behind her.

"It won't work. It occurred to me you might try to call for help. I disconnected it."

Ian had seen her from the window of the study. He might have thought nothing was strange except that she seemed to be in a hurry and when she looked back at the house several times, he became suspicious.

He could not believe that she would actually try to pilot the *Queen Bea,* but she might take a chance on one of the smaller vessels. He had no idea of the extent of her knowledge of boating. The fact that she had boarded the *Queen Bea* suggested she was not totally unfamiliar with boats. Although there was only a remote possibility that she would attempt to leave the island on her own, she could easily call for help.

"How did you know what I was doing? Have you taken to spying on my every move?"

"No, I just happened to see you from the window of the study. You were obviously up to something, you were in such a hurry."

He took the receiver from her hand and replaced it. Zoe could think of nothing more to say. She was angry, to say the least. She was also embarrassed at being caught. She turned away from the telephone, brushed past him, and almost ran back to the house.

Derek watched from the hallway as she entered and went directly to her room. He met Ian in the living room when he entered a few minutes later. His brother had explained what he suspected when he saw her leave. She had appeared to have a specific purpose in mind, not just a leisurely stroll.

"Did she say anything to you?" Ian asked.

"Not a word," Derek replied. "You knew she couldn't use the radio. Why did you bother to go after her?"

"I don't know. I guess I wanted to see for myself that that was what she had in mind. I also wanted to make sure that she wouldn't be so foolish as to actually try to take the boat and attempt to return on her own."

He started down the hall. "Shall we get back to work?"

Zoe spent the remainder of the afternoon in her room. She fumed for a while and finally came to the conclusion that it would serve no purpose to sulk. Besides, she would have to come out eventually, unless she was planning to go on a hunger strike.

The men had disappeared again when she exited the bedroom. She quietly walked to the door and let herself out. This time she wandered over to the gazebo and climbed the stairs. There was a built-in ledge and two small wooden tables inside, as if it was arranged just for quiet moments of rest and contemplation. She sat there for a long while, racking her brain for some clue to her past. She forced herself to stop when she felt the beginnings of a headache.

She returned to the house and went in search of more aspirin. When she returned to the living room, Derek was in the kitchen. Having eaten a late breakfast, she was just now realizing it was close to dinner time.

"I'm afraid you'll be on your own for dinner. Sometimes when Ian gets going with work, you can't even get him away to eat. I'm fixing some sandwiches for us, but you can help yourself to whatever you like."

After he left, Zoe found hamburger patties in the freezer

and the makings for a salad. When she had finished eating
her solitary meal, the men were still closeted in the study.

She wandered outside and again mounted the stairs to
the gazebo. She watched the sun set as a breath of air
wafted through the openings in the structure's railing. The
magnificent colors that painted the sky combined with the
soft breeze caressing her skin and began to work their
magic. After a while, she started to relax and the tension
slowly drained from her body.

She was not surprised that there was still no sign of Ian
and Derek when she entered the house some time later.
Having had little sound sleep the previous night, the easing
of the tension was followed closely by sheer exhaustion.
She headed toward her room and bed. Hopefully, without
being awakened every few hours, she could get a good
night's sleep.


The next morning Zoe awakened feeling almost as
exhausted as she had the night before. She could not lay
the blame at Ian's feet this time. She had slept fitfully,
thanks to her disturbing dreams. She could not remember
them, but she had awakened twice with a feeling of fore-
boding.

She dragged herself out of bed and into the shower.
The water revived her body, if not her spirits. The kitchen
was empty when she entered it, but there was a fresh pot
of coffee and she helped herself. After a breakfast of muffins and juice, she went outside.

The spectacular setting struck her anew as she stood on
the porch. She descended the stairs slowly and walked over
to the gazebo, but instead of climbing the stairs of the
shelter she turned and continued across the lawn and down
to the beach.

She walked as far as the pier and gazed up at the large
vessel that had brought her to the island. The *Queen Bea.*

Who was Bea? She recalled hearing somewhere that men usually named their boats after their wives or girlfriends.

Ian had said the boat belonged to him, but he was wearing no ring. Of course, that was no real proof. A more realistic indication of his single status was that she could not imagine a wife allowing her husband to go off to some island alone for two or three months.

If he had a wife, surely she would have accompanied him—unless they had had some huge disagreement. Her observations of the two brothers did not suggest that likelihood. On the other hand, a girlfriend would have no real control over his decision.

Zoe shook her head, as if to clear it of what she realized were ridiculous speculations. In spite of her efforts to dismiss such thoughts, she could not forget the tingle she had felt when he touched her. She told herself it was because she had been under a strain and was not herself at that time. Reactions like that just did not happen under normal conditions except in novels.

In addition to the yacht and the cabin cruiser, there was a smaller outboard motorboat. She searched her mind for some recollection of boarding the yacht. What reason would she have for even being at the marina? There was no inkling of an explanation. Prior to waking up on the sofa the previous night, her memory was a total blank.

She turned to begin her walk back to the house and was struck by the view of the beautiful structure. The stone and cedar building was breathtaking in itself. It sat on a rise atop stone-faced pillars that, unknown to her, were actually pilings sunk deep into the ground. The practicality did not detract from the beauty of the building that was further enhanced by a profusion of azaleas and bougainvillea on all sides, helping to disguise the pilings.

She had already seen the view afforded by the windows spanning the entire length of the living room. One of the windows to the right of the living room indicated the study in which she had seen Ian and Derek. Of those on the left, she knew one was the powder room she had used shortly after her arrival. The other was probably Ian's bedroom, since she had seen him carry his luggage down the hall the first evening. She guessed that the other windows on the right belonged to additional bedrooms. As if the house was not immense enough, she had already noticed the small bungalow in back of the main structure.

She walked slowly back toward the house. She was captivated by the beauty of the setting and the gentle sound of the waves lapping the beach. The effect it had on her was amazing. She felt quite relaxed. It was hard to sustain her anger in these pleasant surroundings.

When she reached the lawn, Zoe decided she was not ready to go inside the house. The two men were obviously engrossed in business. Judging from the previous day, it was up to her to find a way to fill the time.

Even if they had not been busy, she could not imagine holding an ordinary conversation with them. What did they have to discuss? Ian had made his position clear and she would not allow herself to be reduced to begging.

She settled herself on the stone wall, her eyes on the ocean but not really focused. A slight sound behind her alerted her to Ian's arrival. A moment later, he was sitting beside her.

He had been watching her from the window as she walked to the pier and back. He felt, again, a twinge of guilt. She looked so lost and forlorn.

"We have a small problem to discuss," he told her.

Zoe stared at him. "You have a knack for understatements. Considering the circumstances, it would seem that we have more than a small problem."

Ian ignored her comment. He was determined not to rise to the bait.

"For now, the subject that I'm sure is on your mind, is not open for discussion. Although I hesitate to bring up the other subject, it's a problem we need to discuss. The immediate problem is a name for you, until you regain your memory."

Zoe's eyes reflected her apprehension. She wished she were as confident as he seemed to be.

"I'm sure it's only a matter of time. As I said before, it doesn't appear that your injury was severe enough to have caused permanent damage. Looking at you now, I think it's safe to assume that you don't have a concussion. If we accept that conclusion, it's hard to believe that your injury is really responsible for the amnesia."

"Are you a doctor?"

Ian glanced at her to assure himself that she was not being sarcastic. He had already seen examples of that. Her expression showed only curiosity and it occurred to him that she knew nothing of his profession. He was not sure he wanted to give her that information. On the one hand, it might help to jog her memory. On the other hand, it might be a greater threat to him and his plans.

"No, I'm not a doctor. I have heard of something called hysterical amnesia, however. Its cause is more emotional than physical. It makes sense that, if the amnesia had been caused by your injury, we could expect that you would have a mild concussion, at the least. I think you'll agree that there's no indication of that.

"It appears that even your headache has disappeared. Some small recollection is bound to come and that will be the beginning. It will all start to come back. I know it's easier said than done, but try to relax and think of it as an unplanned vacation."

"You're right. It is easier said than done. First of all, this so-called vacation is not by choice. Aside from the other obvious reasons, spending day after day just looking at the ocean might get a little boring."

Ian ignored her reference to the fact that she was there against her will.

"That's one problem I can solve. We have a few diversions available to relieve the boredom. There's not much in the way of television. Understandably, the normal reception is terrible and I can't bring myself to install a satellite dish out here.

"There are a number of movie videos and music CDs, however. In addition to that, there's a fairly extensive library. I should have given you the tour yesterday. Derek and I were so caught up in our work it didn't occur to me."

He smiled, looking at the ocean. "Of course, there's always the obvious pastime. If you recall, there were a couple of swimsuits in those packages I brought. You can always go swimming."

"I don't swim," she said, flatly.

His smile widened as he appraised her voluptuous curves. "In that case, you can just sunbathe."

"Haven't you heard that the sun's rays can be harmful to one's health?"

Ian chuckled. "Alright, I give up. I won't make any other suggestions."

Zoe thought about her earlier statement and wrinkled her forehead. "That's strange. I don't know how I know that I can't swim."

"That's what I mean. It's probably as I suggested. The memories will start trickling back, little by little."

He paused. "We still haven't solved the immediate problem. What do you suggest I call you?"

Zoe's expression became serious. "I don't know. It doesn't really matter."

"Well, how about something simple, like Mary? Although you don't really look like a Mary."

Some subtle change in her expression caught his attention. "What is it? Do you remember something?"

Zoe shook her head. "No. I had a fleeting thought, but I can't get a handle on it."

He touched her hand, gently. "Don't try to force it. It'll come on its own."

When he touched her, Zoe felt the tingle again, like a

prickle of awareness, or anticipation. So much for blaming her reaction on her dazed condition the previous night.

"I walked down to the dock again earlier. I didn't go aboard this time. I hoped that just looking at the yacht more closely again would trigger that small recollection you mentioned. Obviously, I didn't waste time touring it yesterday. Would it be alright if I went aboard now? Maybe that would help."

Ian shrugged. "I don't see why not," he agreed, jumping down from the stone wall. "I'll come with you."

Before Zoe could make a move to get down herself, his hands came around her waist. Her hands automatically came up to clasp his shoulders, as if to keep herself from falling. It was unnecessary.

He lifted her easily from her perch and set her on the sand. Their eyes met—velvety, chocolate brown and gleaming onyx. Neither seemed able or willing to break the mysterious connection. They stood frozen to the spot for an endless moment.

A group of seagulls landed a short distance away, breaking the spell. He glanced at the noisy birds and, reluctantly, dropped his hands from her waist. Zoe released his shoulders and stepped back. She avoided his eyes, her hands now clasped in front of her. Ian took hold of one hand, freeing it from its mate.

"Shall we go and see if we can shake loose some memories?"

# CHAPTER SEVEN

When they reached the dock, Zoe hesitated. She looked at the vessel for a few minutes, but received no more of a glimmer than she had on her previous visits. Ian urged her aboard, holding on to her hand as she stepped onto the deck.

He led her downstairs to the lounge. Zoe walked slowly across the velvety beige carpet that cushioned the entire floor. She looked around at the plush but unfamiliar furnishings. The cinnamon-colored armchairs that complimented the striped sofa were arranged on one side of the room opposite a cabinet that contained a television. Through the doorway behind a bar at the far end of the salon she glimpsed a stove and part of a table.

"Where was I when you found me?"

"Over here," he said, walking past her to the side of the lounge opposite the galley. He descended the few stairs, opened the door, and stood waiting for her. Zoe followed, looking down at him. He indicated the area of the hall just at the foot of the stairs.

"You were lying on the floor. From the appearance of

it, we thought you might have hit your head on the stairs themselves, or the corner of the doorjamb, possibly when the yacht lurched as we pulled away from the dock."

Zoe made her way down the stairs. She looked down the hall and then up at him, questioningly.

"Help yourself. Check the rooms."

She started slowly down the hall. He propped the door open and sat down on the stairs, quietly watching. She entered one room after the other, her forehead wrinkling with the effort of trying to remember.

He had very little doubt now that her amnesia was real. Unfortunately, that did not explain her reasons for being aboard the *Queen Bea.*

After a while, she returned to the stairs where he sat waiting patiently. He stood up as she approached. The look of frustration and fear in her eyes was almost his undoing. She shook her head and his arm came around her shoulders. He could think of nothing to say, no way to console her.

"Let's go," he murmured, urging her up the stairs ahead of him.

As they walked along the beach toward the house, Zoe forced herself to shake off her dark mood. She looked around her, focusing on the beautiful setting. It would do her no good to brood about her situation. As they neared the house, she looked back at the yacht one last time. She recalled her earlier speculations concerning the boat's name.

"Where did you get the name? I assume it's for someone named Beatrice."

Ian smiled for the first time since they had left the house. He was glad that her mind was temporarily fixed on a topic other than her dilemma.

"You're right. It's named after my grandmother, my mother's mother."

"Is she still alive?"

He nodded, chuckling. "Oh, yes, eighty-two years old and

still going strong. She's a very sweet lady, but she's also very much the queen of the family. Don't misunderstand me, she's earned every bit of it. She raised two children alone after my grandfather died. With her encouragement and support, they both managed to graduate from college.

"And, as if that wasn't a big enough accomplishment, she managed to hold on to this island when so many people were losing their land. She was determined to retain the birthright that had been passed down to my grandfather."

"Has she been aboard?"

He looked down at her, "From what I've just told you about her determination, what do you think? My father tried to talk her out of it, but he made the mistake of referring to her age. Her only reply was, 'It's named after me, I'm going onboard.'

"After that, my father knew that it was a lost cause. Not only did she go on its maiden voyage, she christened it."

"She sounds like a wonderful woman," Zoe murmured.

Ian stopped walking and came around in front of her. He took her by the shoulders and she looked up at him.

"It will come back."

She nodded, but still looked uncertain. Ian felt an unexplainable urge to erase the sad look from her face.

"Let's go back to the house, Gertie. I'll show you the library."

"My name's not Gertie."

"See, you remembered that. Just as you remembered that you don't swim."

Her expression brightened a little. Maybe he was right. Maybe she was trying to rush it. She had to believe that it was just a matter of time.

Taking her hand, Ian continued walking. He could not know what she was feeling. He tried to imagine how he would feel if his memory was erased—to recall nothing of family or friends, or even his own name. He had no intention of sending her back to Savannah with Derek, but he would make an effort to be more pleasant. She was facing enough problems without adding his antagonism to them.

When they entered the house, Derek was sitting at the kitchen table. He studied their expressions as they came through the living room. The fact that Ian still had Zoe's hand clasped in his piqued his interest. Their expressions were even more interesting.

He had no idea what had taken place between them. Knowing his brother, he was sure he had not changed his mind about allowing her to leave the island. It was obvious to him, however, that the animosity had vanished, at least for the time being. More than that, there was a subtle change in their attitudes that indicated more than just a truce.

"Are you ready for lunch?" Ian asked Zoe. "There are cold cuts or tuna, or the makings for a salad," he informed her. "You can help yourself."

"I'd rather see the library, first, if you don't mind."

"Sure, this way."

As it turned out, it was the room next to her bedroom. She had seen the other set of doors when she was on the deck, but assumed it was another bedroom.

They entered the room he called the library. It was aptly named. She was amazed at the collection of books. Floor-to-ceiling bookcases covered two walls and either side of the oak-stained French doors on the third wall. On the wall to the right was a built-in entertainment center that encased a television, a stereo system, and shelves filled with video tapes. He was right. This should certainly be sufficient to keep her from becoming bored.

She wandered over to the shelves, examining the books. There was definitely a wide assortment of topics, including new releases as well as classics, and volumes of everything in between.

She walked over to the doors and looked out on a view

of the ocean identical to that visible from her room. Until she had stepped out on the deck that morning, she had not realized that the house sat on a piece of land that jutted out from the main area of the island. It was situated to afford views of the water from three sides of the structure. The bungalow she had glimpsed from her room and during her walk on the beach was more visible from this vantage point.

"Who lives in that house?"

"My aunt, my father's sister, and her husband. They act as caretakers when there's no one else on the island."

"Are they here?" she asked, hopefully.

She did not have to wait a few days to determine whether it was as deserted as it appeared. When he told her the identity of the occupants, it occurred to her that she might enlist their aid. An older couple such as he described would certainly not approve of his keeping her here against her will.

"No," he replied, guessing the reason for her interest. "They're away for a few months, visiting relatives."

"Oh," she replied, obviously disheartened.

Ian decided it was best to change the subject. His voice broke into her contemplation. "Are you ready for lunch?"

"Yes, I'll be there in a few minutes."

Ian left her alone and joined his brother in the kitchen. He helped himself to a cup of the fresh coffee Derek had brewed. Taking a sip of his drink, he turned and leaned against the counter.

"I took her down to the *Queen Bea*. For what it's worth, I have to concede to your opinion, little brother. I agree that the amnesia is for real. She was very disappointed that being onboard did nothing to jog her memory."

"But that isn't enough for you to let her return to Savannah with me, is it?"

"No," Ian replied. "I can't. Not until I know why she was aboard the *Queen Bea* in the first place."

Zoe entered the kitchen a moment later. Once again,

she had the impression that she had interrupted a discussion that centered around her. She knew if she thought about that for long she would only become angry and frustrated, so she set her suspicions aside and went to prepare something to eat.

After lunch, the men returned to the study and Zoe was left to her own devices. She found a mystery novel, but could not decide whether to settle down in the library or on the deck. She remembered the inviting structure on the front lawn.

After pouring herself a glass of lemonade, she started toward the front door. When she had left the house earlier, she had noticed a collection of family photographs hanging on the wall and scattered atop the credenza near the foyer. This time she paused a moment to examine a few of the pictures.

She recognized Ian's grandmother immediately. Holding the photograph in her hand, she examined the features more closely. Even if Ian had not told her about this proud matriarch, the elderly woman's countenance would have revealed the determination in her personality. She gently returned it to its place on the credenza and continued through the foyer.

Once outside, she paused again, breathing deeply the clean salt air. She strolled slowly across the lawn and climbed the stairs to the gazebo. Placing the glass on one of the tables, she reclined against the pillows on the cushioned ledge. Comfortably ensconced, she settled down to enjoy the novel, to the accompaniment of the sound of lapping waves. She managed to finish two chapters before the soothing sound lulled her to sleep.

Almost two hours had passed before Zoe awakened. Unaware that she was being observed, she stretched slowly. She was totally ignorant of the sensuality of her movements. Ian cleared his throat and her head jerked up off the pillow.

"I'm sorry. I didn't mean to startle you."

She sat up, her hand covering her mouth as she attempted to stifle a yawn. Pivoting her body on the ledge, she turned her legs to the side and planted her feet on the floor before leaning over to retrieve the book that had fallen from her hand while she slept.

Her unexpected movement caused Ian to question the wisdom of coming to look for her. Of course, he had never expected to find her asleep. He certainly had not expected to feel the stirrings of desire when she stretched upon awakening.

He was unable to tear his eyes away from her legs when she turned to sit up. When she leaned over to retrieve the novel, his lower body tightened in response to the glimpse of her full, round breasts. He took a deep breath and focused on her face.

"Did you enjoy your nap?"

"Yes, as a matter of fact, I did. I didn't intend to fall asleep. I guess I can blame it on the sound of the ocean."

Ian smiled. "I imagine you didn't really sleep well last night, being in a strange bed. And, of course, the night before you weren't really allowed to get an uninterrupted night's sleep."

"Now that you mention it, I'm sure that contributed to it," she agreed. "As exhausted as I was yesterday, I guess last night's sleep wasn't enough."

She stood up and stretched again, before turning her back to him to fluff the pillow and cushions where she had been napping. Ian was beginning to have second thoughts about keeping her on the island for two or three months. The possibility of finding himself in the position of fighting physical desire for a woman he had met less than twenty-four hours earlier had never entered his mind.

He stared at the expanse of brown skin exposed by the scoop neck of her dress. His hand itched to touch it, to see if it was as silky smooth as it looked. As if that were not enough, his gaze traveled down to her rounded derriere. He shook his head as if to clear his mind of temptation.

He silently admonished himself. Surely he could spend a
few short months in the same household with a stranger
without losing control. When she turned and smiled, he
was not so sure. He considered his peace of mind would
have been better served by maintaining the original antagonism instead of making efforts to negotiate a truce.

Unaware of his scrutiny, Zoe picked up her glass and
moved toward the steps. Ian was reluctant to let her go,
but could think of no excuse to keep her there. In light
of his latest discovery, he acknowledged it was probably
just as well. He followed her to the house, hanging back
far enough to enjoy the sight of her swaying hips as she
made her way across the lawn.

# CHAPTER EIGHT

Within a few days of her arrival, Zoe had settled into a routine of sorts. There had been no change in her mental state, but she had stopped agonizing over it. She had had a few dreams, but could not remember anything of importance when she awakened. In fact, she remembered nothing of the dreams themselves, only feelings. Some of them had evoked a measure of fear, but of what, she had no idea. Fortunately, none of them had been as terrifying as the ones she had her first night on the island.

She spent most of the day strolling the beach until the sun rose high and became unbearable. She would then move to the shelter of the gazebo where she usually read one of the books from the library. She had not fallen asleep there since that first day. She had become accustomed to her surroundings and was sleeping better at night, in spite of the dreams.

There were times when she did nothing but watch the waves and the seagulls. She saw little of the two men, even at mealtimes.

At one point, Zoe considered enlisting Derek's aid. She

had sensed that he was not in agreement with his brother's decision to keep her on the island. However, after closely observing the interaction of the two men, she was convinced that whatever conflict they might have over her presence on the island, Derek would not take any action without Ian's consent.

As he had planned, Derek left the island a few days after his arrival. After his departure, Zoe's routine remained much the same. Ian spent most of the day in his study with the door closed. For the most part, she was left to fill in the hours with whatever amusement suited her.

Although he was usually busy working in his study when she had breakfast and lunch, he always joined her for dinner. Not only that, he always cooked the evening meal himself. She wondered if he considered this chore his sole responsibility since it was his home.

That attitude might be expected if she were a guest, but that was hardly the case. Under the circumstances, it would have made more sense to leave her to fend for herself, as she had before Derek left. The entire situation was filled with contradictions. Contrary to what she had expected, since that first day when he had indicated his unbending decision, his behavior and attitude toward her were quite pleasant. It was very confusing.

His habit of cooking dinner continued for a week before she decided to take it into her own hands to change it. If nothing else, it would be one more activity to occupy her time.

She returned from a stroll on the beach a little earlier than usual, with the idea of preparing their meal. She entered the house to find him already at work in the kitchen. He paused in his preparations just long enough to acknowledge her presence. She stood in the doorway watching him for a while, before she spoke.

"I do remember how to cook, you know."

Ian smiled. "I'm sure you do, but it's not necessary."

Zoe returned his smile. "Are you afraid I might poison you?"

"That possibility hadn't occurred to me until you mentioned it," he said, looking her directly in the eye. Zoe laughed.

"The reason I haven't asked you to cook is that I was afraid you might feel compelled to agree. At the least, it might lead you to think that I subscribe to the chauvinist attitude that cooking is woman's work."

"I didn't offer to take over completely, only to lend a hand."

"Alright," he acquiesced. "You can finish this salad while I take care of the steaks."

When the salad was done, Zoe set the table. A short time later they sat down to their meal. They had shared meals before and, in spite of the circumstances, those times were pleasant.

Their previous conversations had always been restricted to general topics, such as books, music, favorite movies. She had been surprised at the things she remembered. Unfortunately, recalling favorite books and movies was of little use and did nothing to improve her memory of more important data. This time, Zoe decided she wanted more personal information about him.

"Tell me about your family. I know you have a brother and a sister and an eighty-two-year-old grandmother. What about the rest of your family?"

"Are you sure you want to hear this, Gertie?"

Zoe rolled her eyes at him. He had been calling her by that name since the day after her arrival. Much to her chagrin, she was beginning to get used to it.

"Yes, I want to hear it. Just because I can't remember my own family yet, doesn't mean I'm too sensitive to listen to you talk about yours. I've seen the pictures on the credenza. They are very interesting. Besides, maybe hearing about your family will jolt some memory of my own family."

"My sister's name is Elizabeth. She's an investment broker in Philadelphia. As I explained before, she leaves a few clothes here and the bathroom is always stocked with the necessities. She finds it convenient in case she wants to pick up and leave at a moment's notice. This way, when she gets a few days break, she can get away with little preparation."

One word in his sentence stood out in Zoe's mind. She put her fork down and rested her hand on the table.

"Philadelphia," she murmured.

Ian looked at her closely. "Does that mean something to you?"

Zoe shook her head. "No. I don't know. It's like before. Like it should mean something, but I can't get a handle on it. I can't imagine that I live there. What would I be doing in Georgia, alone?"

Ian lifted her hand from its resting place and held it in his. Unconsciously, his thumb caressed the back of her hand. She looked into his eyes and something there, coupled with the stroking, made her heartbeat quicken.

"Even little clues like that are a good sign. Your mind recognizes something familiar. Eventually, you'll recall why it's familiar," he assured her.

Ian had only meant to offer her encouragement. He would never have imagined that simply touching her would arouse the feelings he had been trying to ignore. After that day in the gazebo, he had kept his distance. Maybe, subconsciously, he had known what a little touch could do.

At the moment, Zoe was as concerned about her own reaction to his touch as she was about regaining her memory. She cleared her throat, gently pulling her hand from his. Her heartbeat slowly settled back into its normal rhythm as they picked up their utensils and continued eating. Ian continued the conversation.

"My parents live just outside of Savannah. Both of them are retired now. My grandmother, Beatrice, lives with them. It took a few years of cajoling before she agreed to that living arrangement."

"You've already told me you're not a doctor. What do you do?"

"I own a software design company," he informed her, after a moment's hesitation. "I also do some consulting work."

He watched closely for some flicker of recollection when he mentioned software design. There was nothing in her expression to hint at anything more than curiosity.

Some nuance in his voice alerted Zoe to his reluctance to go into any further detail. She could not imagine why he would not want to discuss his work, but it was not important enough to her to press for further information.

"Derek told me this island was passed down in your family from your great-great-grandfather," she said, changing the subject.

"That's right. I don't think it ever had an official name. It does show up on some of the maps, but only as a small dot of land about five miles from the mainland. It's always been referred to simply as Blake's Island since that was my great-great-grandfather's name."

They finished their meal and worked together cleaning up. He had just finished placing their glasses in the dishwasher when he turned to see her stretching to reach one of the higher shelves for a container. The short sundress was raised to mid-thigh by her action, and Ian froze. Her struggle to reach the shelf finally brought him to his senses, and he went to her aid.

His response to a simple touch during their meal was minor compared to his body's reaction now. That incident brought about a change in his plans for the evening. While they were eating, he had been mentally making plans to spend it with her instead of closed up in his study, maybe watching a movie. Now it did not seem wise to spend the evening in such close proximity. He excused himself after dinner and retired to his study.

It did him little good to hide behind closed doors. The old adage, "out of sight, out of mind," was not working. The tempting visions of shapely legs and lushly rounded breasts and hips did nothing for his concentration.

He tried to write it off as the normal reaction of an average red-blooded male to a warm, physically attractive female. He might have been able to convince himself of that if it were only a physical reaction, but it was more than that. It was even more than just an understandable compassion because of her amnesia. The growing feelings of protectiveness could not be explained by compassion or physical desire.

He could not even claim it was a rebound from his ill-fated engagement. After all, it was not as though he had been sitting at home for two years twiddling his thumbs. He had dated several attractive women since that time and he had felt some measure of physical desire for all of them. None of them, though, had affected him as instantly, or as intensely, as she had in such a few days.


Sitting across the hall in the library, Zoe was having her own problems with concentration. She had tried reading to no avail. After reading the same page three times, she gave up. She sorted through the movie videos, found an adventure thriller and popped it into the machine, thinking that the fast-paced action would hold her attention. She managed no better with the movie than she had with the book.

Her thoughts strayed to the man behind the closed door and the feelings he evoked. She was concerned about her reactions to him for a number of reasons. Not the least of these was the realization that she had no idea if there was another man in her life.

She supposed that she could be reasonably certain that there was no husband—she was wearing no ring. Most likely, that also meant she was not engaged either.

Zoe mulled over the questions running through her mind. Her fascination with him was more than a mere appreciation for a charming man, although he was, indeed, charming. She had felt his allure even in the beginning, in spite of the antagonism.

With all her speculation, she could only come to one conclusion. The most realistic solution would be to accept her obvious attraction to Ian as a sign. How could she have any deep feelings for another man and react physically to him the way she did? How could she even be thinking these things? Surely, she was not that fickle? Even with a loss of memory, how could she not remember being in love?

That unpleasant thought brought another question to mind. If she had been involved with another man, would she feel differently about Ian when she regained her memory?

Her thoughts went around and around. In the end, she gave up trying to analyze the situation. First and foremost, she needed to remind herself that this man was keeping her isolated on an island. It was also important that she remember that she knew very little about him, except what he chose to tell her.

In opposition to those reminders, one thought stayed in the back of her mind. It was hard to believe that the concern he had shown was not genuine. She was also beginning to think that his feelings toward her involved more than empathy for what she might be experiencing because of the amnesia.

When the closing credits of the movie began rolling, Zoe was taken by surprise. She realized that if anyone had asked her, she would be able to tell them very little about the story. All she recalled was something about plans being stolen and everyone looking for the thief. In other words, a typical spy thriller.

After rewinding the tape and returning it to its place in the cabinet, she yawned and stretched. What they said about salt air being relaxing must be true. If nothing else, she was certainly catching up on her rest here on this island.

She turned off the television and the lights and went to her room. After a luxurious bubble bath, she went to bed. Even in her sleep she could not escape Ian. Her dreams were the most pleasant she'd had since her arrival, filled with images of him.

The next morning after breakfast, Zoe took her usual walk on the beach. This time she went farther afield and explored the woods a short distance from the house. As she walked through the brush, the sweet smell of sea grass permeated her nostrils. The Spanish moss trailing from the live oaks formed a filmy curtain around her as she picked her way over shells and driftwood. She found an old log, surprisingly clean, and sat down to enjoy the smells and the sound of the ocean. It really was a lovely place. Under other circumstances, she could enjoy spending an extended period of time on this island.

When Ian had refused to let her leave the island, he had assured her that she was safe. The strange thing was that she believed that. Whatever his reasons for keeping her here, he had given her no reason to think he meant her any harm. At first she questioned her own judgment in trusting him, but the more contact she had with him, the more she was convinced she had no reason to be afraid of him.

# CHAPTER NINE

Zoe lost track of time, sitting there in the woods. It was not until the sun began peeping through the moss directly overhead that she became aware of the passage of time. The sun told her that it must be close to noon, which meant she had been sitting there for well over two hours. She had left her hat behind at the house and as the sun broke through the filmy ceiling, its rays became uncomfortable. She stood up and started back through the brush.

She had only walked a short distance along the beach when she saw a bird lying near an outcrop of rocks closer to the house. She ran over and knelt down beside it. The pitiful creature was barely breathing. Zoe had no idea what to do for it. She ran back to the house for help, hoping Ian could offer some suggestion.

He was nowhere in sight. It was not hard to guess his whereabouts. The study door was closed, as she expected. No doubt he was still at work. She knocked, but did not wait for an invitation to enter. Her distress was obvious to Ian when she opened the door.

"What is it? What's the matter?" he asked, rising from his chair.

"There's a seagull on the beach. It's hurt."

"A what?" he asked, frowning.

Zoe guessed from his expression that he probably thought she was overreacting. An injured bird was, obviously, not important enough to have his work interrupted.

She shrugged. "A seagull. I thought you might know how to help it."

He came around the side of the desk and gestured for her to lead the way. Zoe ran out of the house and across the lawn. Not bothering to use the steps, she jumped down from the wall and ran the short distance to where the bird lay.

Ian was right behind her. He was more concerned with her reaction than with the bird itself. When he reached the bird, his heart sank. He knelt beside her and examined it more closely.

"I'm afraid it's too late, Gertie. He's dead."

She looked up at him in disbelief. Then she looked back at the still little creature. Tears formed in her eyes and she tried surreptitiously to wipe them away.

"I'm sorry," he murmured.

She shook her head in an effort to dismiss the sadness she felt. "It doesn't matter. It's just a bird," she insisted.

Ian took her by the hand and stood up, drawing her up off her knees. His arms came around her and she leaned into him.

"It does matter. And it's okay to be upset. In fact, if more people became upset whenever an animal died, this might be a better world."

He set her away from him and wiped the remaining tears from her cheeks. Then he gently kissed her forehead. When he looked down at her again, their eyes met. Zoe licked her suddenly dry lips. It was almost his undoing. Before he could act on his impulse, the spell was broken by her words.

"I know it probably sounds childish, but can we bury him?"

"It doesn't sound childish at all. I'm sorry if I sounded impatient when you came to me for help. I'll go and get a spade."

When he returned, he carried the bird into the woods. Zoe chose a spot beneath one of the weeping willows and he started digging. A short time later, they were walking back to the house, hand in hand.

"I'm sorry I interrupted your work. I didn't know what else to do."

Ian looked down at her. "The interruption was no big deal. It's almost time for lunch, anyway."

Ian returned to his study after lunch and Zoe took her book out to the gazebo. After the morning's events, she should have known her concentration would be no better than it had been the previous evening. It seemed she could still feel his warm lips on her forehead.

That evening Ian finally gave in to the temptation he had been fighting for days. At his suggestion, they adjourned to the den to watch a movie after dinner. In reality, he was more occupied with watching her than with watching the movie. In an effort to keep the mood light, he had chosen a comedy. It was good to hear her laugh. Even in the midst of her personal problems, she still had the ability to appreciate humor. It told him that she had managed to retain her spirit.

He had already seen evidence of her strength in her ability to accept her amnesia without falling apart. He would have expected at least a minor episode of hysterics by now. Even assuming that she believed it was temporary, it was undoubtedly a frightening situation. Add that to the fact that she was being held against her will, and her ability to retain her composure was even more amazing.

It occurred to him that her acceptance of that particular

aspect indicated that she trusted him. He told himself that was only because she did not remember who she was, or why she had been hiding on his yacht. Somewhere in the recesses of her mind there must be some knowledge of his identify and background. Why else would she have chosen the *Queen Bea?*

On the other hand, if she trusted him, why would she have been hiding, unless she was spying on him? Whatever her feelings had been when she boarded the yacht, she showed no signs of fear now. In fact, she had settled rather comfortably into her present surroundings. When it came right down to it, he had to admit he had not given her much choice. But then, she had not put up a great deal of protest since that first day. The idea that she trusted him gave rise to a twinge of guilt. In spite of everything, she trusted him.

Her laughter periodically cut into his thoughts. From all appearances it seemed that she was not as concerned about discovering her identity as he was. If he had not seen her distress, he might have questioned the validity of her loss of memory. If it was an act, she deserved an award.

There were other questions he had been turning over in his mind. She had not been dressed for sneaking around on a yacht, which was in her favor. On the other hand, she was mysteriously devoid of any form of identification. It was all very puzzling.

For now he had to set those questions aside. He had more important matters to consider. In spite of his speculations, he had reached only one conclusion. He could not allow her to leave until his questions were answered. Eventually, he would have his answers, even if she did not regain her memory.

Ian had been so caught up in his reflections that before he knew it, the movie had ended and Zoe had the remote control in her hand, rewinding the tape.

Until then, Zoe had been engrossed in the movie and totally unaware of his perusal. When she turned to face him, she recalled her earlier apprehension when he had suggested this activity.

Ian smiled and her pulse quickened. There was something about the look in his eyes that seemed to be affecting her ability to breath.

"Judging from your laughter, I assume you enjoyed the movie."

With some effort, Zoe found her voice. "Yes, I did."

Tearing her eyes from his, she stood up and walked over to the television. Putting some distance between them helped her regain her senses.

"You have quite a collection here," she observed, her voice still a little shaky.

She kept her back to him as she scanned the titles. Maybe, if she avoided looking into those ebony eyes, she could convince herself that the heart palpitations were a figment of her imagination.

Using his own feelings as a gauge, Ian guessed that she was also struggling with her emotions. He might have thought that this idea was only wishful thinking if it were not for her expressive eyes. He wondered if she was aware of the desire that was evident when she looked at him. The same desire that he knew must be reflected in his own eyes.

"Yes. We usually spend a good deal of time here, off and on. Since the television reception is very limited, videos are the next best thing. I have a few younger cousins who visit occasionally and the movies protect us from constant loud music."

Zoe summoned her courage and turned to face him. "Do they enjoy reading? You have almost everything imaginable in that department, too."

"As a matter of fact, they're avid readers. However, for some reason, teenagers seem to think that reading has to be accompanied by music."

She smiled and stifled a yawn. That action gave her the perfect excuse to make her escape. Without a movie to distract them, it would probably not take much for the desire that simmered just below the surface to reach the boiling point. The vision evoked by that possibility was tempting, but she was not prepared to cope with it. It was too soon.

"I think there must be some kind of tranquilizer in salt air. I guess I'll call it a day."

Walking over to the table, she retrieved the novel she had been reading earlier that day. Ian had another glimpse of tempting full breasts and silently agreed that her decision was probably a wise one.

He nodded. They said their good nights and Zoe left the room.

# CHAPTER TEN

The next week was quiet and uneventful. In the first couple of weeks, Zoe had remained fairly calm. In spite of her doubts, she had made herself believe that Ian and Derek were right, her memory would return.

She had been on the island a month now, and she was beginning to feel more anxious. She supposed a month was not really a great deal of time, but she thought it should be enough for some recollection to surface. She had remembered nothing, not even her name.

Ian had noticed a change in her in the past two weeks. She very seldom smiled anymore, and he could see that she was rapidly losing her optimism. He had started seriously considering taking her back to Savannah.

Although he did not expect that she would miraculously regain her memory simply by returning to the city, there might be some way to discover her identity. He still was not comfortable with the idea of allowing her to leave the island without knowing why she had been aboard the *Queen Bea*. However, if it was a matter of letting her go or watching her sink into depression, he would have no choice.

His decision was made for him. After watching her brood, he was surprised when she walked into the kitchen one morning with a heart-stopping smile on her face. She walked over to the counter and poured a mug of coffee before turning to face him.

"My name is Zoe," she announced.

"What?"

"I said, my name is Zoe." She took a sip of coffee.

"Do you remember anything else?"

"No. I don't even remember my last name, just Zoe."

Ian hesitated. She looked so happy. He did not want to be responsible for bursting her bubble, but he had to ask more questions.

"How do you know? How can you be so sure?"

She shrugged. "I just know. I had a dream last night. I can't remember much, only that a voice was calling for 'Zoe' and I knew that was me."

"Maybe the name came from something you've read, or is just a name you've heard."

Zoe could not believe her ears. "Why are you doing this?"

Ian sighed. He swiveled his chair around so that he was now facing her.

"I'm not trying to undermine your conviction, I'm just trying to help you understand that just because you dreamed it doesn't mean it was you they were calling."

"I realize that. I just know it's my name. Why is that so unbelievable. You said it yourself, that the memories would start trickling back little by little."

"I know I told you that and I think that's true. It's just that, for one thing, Zoe's a very unusual name. I mean, be realistic. It's hard to believe that, in this day and age, any African-American mother would name her daughter 'Zoe.' "

As soon as the words left his mouth, he knew it was a mistake. If he'd had any doubts, the anger in her eyes would have made it very clear before she said a word.

She moved away from the counter and walked toward him. She stopped directly in front of him, her hands on her hips.

"I don't know," she said, her voice deceptively soft. "Maybe the same kind that would name her son 'Ian.' "

Ian felt his anger rising. It was on the tip of his tongue to explain that the name Ian was an old family name that had been passed down to some child in the family for generations. Usually, the child was fortunate enough to have it as a middle name that was never used. He hesitated a moment and his anger dissipated. He saw the situation from her perspective.

Ian chuckled, holding his hands up in defense. "Touché," he murmured.

Zoe relaxed her stance. He had taken her by surprise for the second time since she'd walked into the kitchen. She had not expected his skepticism when she announced her discovery. She had certainly not expected his surrender when she attacked his own name.

"I hope you know that I meant no insult to your parents. You just took me totally by surprise. And you have to admit, it is an unusual name. Maybe even more unusual than Ian. Or, maybe it's a toss-up between the two."

She returned his smile and backed up a few steps. She retrieved her mug of coffee from the counter and returned to join him at the table.

"Zoe," he murmured, nodding. "Actually, it suits you."

She sipped her coffee. "Does that mean I'm unusual, too?"

"As a matter of fact, I had already reached that conclusion. One day I'll explain the reason for that opinion."

Zoe sighed. "I just wish I could remember more of the dream."

"It's a start, Zoe."

"I know, I know. I keep reminding myself of that."

"I just have one more question."

"What? I don't really have any more answers."

He grinned. "You can answer this. Does this mean I have to stop calling you Gertie?"

"Yes!" she said emphatically.

She had to admit, though, some part of her would miss it. She had come to regard it as a term of endearment, although she would never admit it to anyone, even herself.

After breakfast, they took a walk on the beach. Zoe asked to be taken to the yacht. She had hoped that now that she knew her name, it might jog loose some other memories. She went through each of the rooms, even the galley.

Even when he described the area where the yacht had been moored, she recalled nothing. There was no hint of an answer to any of the dozens of questions running through her mind.

She had told him she could not swim. She recalled that. So, why in the world would she have chosen to come aboard a boat? And why would she have been hiding? She felt the beginnings of a headache and willed herself to stop worrying about it. She knew her name. That was enough for now.

When they returned to the house, they went their separate ways. Ian retired to his study, and Zoe took her novel out to the gazebo.

Ian was aware that the fact that she had an unusual name was in his favor. It meant he would not have to return her to the mainland. He could put Jared to work.

If he gave him a first name and a description, he might be able to come up with a possible identification. Of course, a photo would be even better. He had to try to take a snapshot of her without her being aware of what he was doing. If she knew he had taken a picture, it would not take much for her to guess that it could be used to help her.

He knew that she often took walks on the beach alone. He had noticed she had a book with her when she left the house a few minutes earlier, which probably meant she was in the gazebo at the moment. He would have to be alert for the right time.

The perfect opportunity presented itself sooner than he expected. That afternoon, as Zoe was taking one of her walks on the beach he decided that it was probably the best chance he would have to take her picture without her being aware of it.

He pulled out his camera and fitted it with the telephoto lens. He managed to get several shots from a variety of angles before she started walking back toward the gazebo.

He had already arranged to meet with Derek and Jared in Savannah in two days time. Jared was a good detective and he had connections. Ian was hopeful that his friend would come up with more information about his guest.

The day of Ian's trip to the mainland, Zoe awakened with a feeling that something was amiss. She donned her robe and went to the kitchen. There was a pot of coffee, still warm, but no sign of Ian.

She assumed he was locked away in his study until the sheet of paper lying on the table drew her attention. It was a note from him explaining that he had gone to the mainland to replenish their grocery supplies. The note promised he would return before dark. She supposed that was meant to comfort her, although she could not imagine why he bothered.

If the object of her anger had been in sight, she'd have gone into a rage. As it was, she decided she did not want to waste a tirade on an empty room.

Since he had seen fit to desert her without even having the courage to tell her to her face, she would put the time to good use. It was time to see what was so secret in that study of his.

She marched down the hall, tried the door, and discovered it was locked. She should have guessed he would never leave it unprotected. She was twice as angry as she had been before, but she forced herself to calm down. She would be ready for him when he returned.

Derek and Jared were already seated when Ian arrived at the restaurant. He greeted the two men and sat down, pulling the roll of film from his pocket.

"I assume Derek filled you in on the latest developments."

"Yeah. He also told me about your uninvited guest. I have to ask you, man. Are you sure keeping her there is a good idea? You're an intelligent man, so I'm sure I don't have to explain the possible legal repercussions."

"For now, I don't have much choice. Besides, depending on her reason for being aboard the *Queen Bea,* the repercussions might be more serious for her than for me."

He paused to give the proper weight to his next statement. His two companions exchanged glances. Derek had already warned Jared that trying to convince him to return their guest to Savannah was a lost cause.

"By the way, her name is Zoe. I don't have a last name, but I managed to get a few snapshots of her. Maybe, with the help of some of your contacts, you can come up with a last name."

Derek was the first to respond. "She remembered?"

"Yes. It seemed a little unbelievable to me, at first. It is an unusual name, but she seems certain. She's recalled a few bits and pieces, but nothing else of value."

Ian turn to Jared. "The fact that it's an unusual name should be of some help to you, even without a last name to go with it."

Jared nodded. "If nothing else, I can do a little discreet digging to see if there appears to be any connection to our friend. I'll check with the police to see if there's a missing person report on a woman that fits her description.

As soon as you're ready, we can proceed with the next step."

"Well, I expect to be ready for that in a month or so."

"What happened?" Derek asked. "I thought you'd have the problems ironed out by now."

He knew his brother well, and there was some subtlety in his voice when he talked about Zoe that had not been there three weeks ago.

He could not say he was totally surprised. He was a little concerned, though. In their present situation, Ian could not afford to become romantically involved with her.

Ian shrugged. "I ran into a problem I hadn't foreseen."

That cryptic remark was the only explanation he offered. He picked up the menu, signaling that the subject was closed. Jared and Derek exchanged glances again, but neither of them made any effort to extract more information.

They finished their meal with no further discussion of Ian's guest. Derek brought Ian up to date on company business, assuring him that the office was running smoothly. As they were leaving the restaurant, Ian called Derek aside.

"I want you to do something for me, if Jared comes up with anything conclusive in the way of an identity. Find out where she lives and see that any rent arrearages are paid up. In fact, pay it for a few months ahead, while you're at it."

Derek looked puzzled. What was Ian up to now?

"I don't understand. What's your point?"

"Think about it, Derek. Even if our suspicions are proven to be true, do we want to be responsible for her being homeless when this is all settled? It would be even worse if we're wrong."

"First of all, I have to take exception to your use of the pronoun 'we.' I agree that everything should be done to see that she's not evicted for being behind in her rent since she doesn't even remember where she lives. That's not the question. If you recall, I'm the one who tried to talk you out of keeping her there in the first place. What I'm trying to understand is the reason for this change of heart."

Ian narrowed his eyes at his brother's reminder, but he could not contradict him. "Let's just say I've had an attack of conscience, and leave it at that."

Ian could hear the knowing smile in his brother's voice when he responded to this statement.

"If you say so."

Ian sighed. "Will you just do that for me?"

"What excuse do you propose I give her landlord? It might not help her reputation to have a strange man paying several months rent for her."

"I'm sure you can come up with something."

"Thanks for the confidence," he replied. The sarcasm in his voice did not escape Ian.

Derek sighed. "I'll take care of it."

"Thanks, Derek. I'll call you next week."

When he left the restaurant, Ian drove to the supermarket in Derek's car. He had left his own vehicle at his parents' home when he'd originally picked up the yacht and it was a little inconvenient carting groceries around in a taxi. They had arranged for Jared to take Derek to the marina later to pick it up.

Before long, Ian was headed back to the island. Jared had promised to let him know if he came up with any information on Zoe. Other than that, there would be no need for the men to meet until Ian had completed his work. He admitted to himself that his work had not proceeded as it should have, thanks to a very distracting young woman.

# CHAPTER ELEVEN

As he pulled up to the dock at Blake's Island, Ian spied Zoe walking on the beach. He had read between the lines of his brother's remark in the restaurant. He was well aware of what was at stake, but he was unwilling to ignore his growing feelings for her.

"Who are you kidding?" he muttered to himself. "Ignoring your feelings doesn't appear to be an option."

Her calm appearance as she strolled the beach did not fool Ian. He knew she would be angry at his abandonment that morning. As he approached, he steeled himself for her tirade.

She greeted him with her hands on her hips and fire in her eyes. He had little hope of soothing her anger, but decided that he might as well give it a try. He still had the same arguments in his favor. Without a name, where would she go?

"I hope you saw my note this morning. I left so early, I didn't want to wake you."

"You really think I'm a fool, don't you? Your unwillingness to awaken me had nothing to do with your early departure."

Ian stood still, watching her. He waited patiently for her to get the anger out of her system. She was entitled to that much. He was surprised when it seemed to suddenly drain from her. Her hands left her hips and spread out, as if in surrender.

"You win—this time. Bear this in mind, though. When I get back to the mainland, and I will get back, you'd better be prepared to hire a good lawyer. Kidnapping is an extremely serious offense. I doubt the FBI will buy your lame excuse that I stowed away on your boat."

She did not wait for a reply. Turning on her heel, she marched off toward the woods. She was in dire need of the quiet solitude she had found there before.

Ian sighed heavily as he watched her go. She was right. He had already heard the same warning from his brother weeks earlier and from Jared a few hours earlier, although they had both expressed it more subtly.

He pushed those thoughts to the back of his mind. As far as he could see, he had no choice but to keep her on the island. When she remembered her name it had restored her spirits and he had discarded any plan to return her to Savannah. Now that she seemed to have overcome the threat of depression, his original plans took precedence over anything else.

There was no further conversation between them for the remainder of the evening. Ian closeted himself in the study and Zoe stayed in her room. She had declined to join him for dinner and, as far as he could tell, had not eaten at all.

When Zoe awakened the next morning, she was starved. She got out of bed and donned her robe.

"That's what happens when you punish yourself by going to bed without dinner," she mumbled to herself.

She was not looking forward to seeing Ian. Her anger had not dissipated completely, but she refused to give him the satisfaction of arguing with him. She wished she could just ignore him, but that was impossible. Even when she retreated to the gazebo or the woods, she was unable to get him out of her mind.

She was grateful to find the kitchen deserted. She had detected sounds of movement in the study and assumed he was hard at work.

He entered the kitchen some time later, as she was finishing a satisfying breakfast of sausages and eggs. He murmured a greeting, which she ignored, and refilled the coffee mug in his hand. Ian turned and leaned back against the counter. His gaze followed her as she rose from the table to place her dishes in the dishwasher. As she walked past him, toward the door, he reached out and stopped her.

"Zoe, I admit you have every reason to be angry. I hope, eventually, you'll understand why this is necessary. Besides, there is still the question of where you would go if I did take you back to the mainland."

"I'm not buying that excuse anymore, Ian. There are ways that I could be helped to discover my identity, especially since I know my first name now."

She glanced at his hand clasping her wrist. "Please, let go of my arm."

Reluctantly, Ian released her. He watched the gentle sway of her hips through the robe as she left the room.

Their paths did not cross again until that evening. Ian was in the process of preparing dinner when Zoe returned from a walk on the beach. She had learned her lesson the day before. She would not go without dinner again.

She entered the kitchen, prepared to cook her own meal. After her fit of temper, she did not expect that he would be willing to share his, but she was mistaken.

"I've steamed the shrimp I bought yesterday. There's

also a seafood salad in the refrigerator, if you would prefer that."

At first he considered her lack of response as normal, considering the disagreements they'd had. After a moment, something in her silence drew his attention. She had a faraway look in her eyes. She looked stricken. He walked over to her.

"Zoe?" he murmured, touching her arm to get her attention. "What is it? What's the matter?"

"I can't eat shrimp. I can't eat any shellfish. I'm allergic, deathly allergic."

She pulled away from him and wandered dazedly to a chair. She hugged her arms to her waist, her shoulders slightly trembling. Ian followed her. He knelt down in front of her.

"Zoe, I think I'm missing something. Why are you so upset about being allergic to shellfish?"

"You don't understand. It's not just a minor allergy. The last time I ate shrimp was when I was a teenager. I had a severe reaction. My throat started to close up and I couldn't breathe."

Her gaze met and held his. "Suppose I hadn't remembered that? Suppose I had eaten those shrimp? I'd have been dead before you could get me to a doctor or a hospital."

Ian's heart wrenched at the picture she painted. "But, you did remember, Zoe. That means that your self-preservation instincts are still intact, in spite of the loss of memory."

As he said the words, he tried to convince himself that it was true. Tears had formed in her eyes. Tears of anxiety and worry. It was obvious that she was close to panic.

"You're just guessing. We can't be sure of that."

He clasped her hands in his. "You're right, Zoe. We can't be certain, but if you think about it, it makes sense. You even remembered exactly when you first discovered the allergy. It's just like when you recalled that you can't swim.''

He held on to her hands with one of his while the other came up to wipe the tears that were now rolling down her cheeks. He could feel the trembling in her fingers. Instinctively, his arms enfolded her.

''It's alright. You're recalling everything, bit by bit. Soon, it will all come back.''

She leaned into his embrace and closed her eyes. The anger was forgotten and the anxiety slowly dissipated. Both emotions were replaced by one that, on a different level, was even more unsettling. This new emotion could also ultimately be her undoing.

She opened her eyes and lifted her hands, placing them on his chest. She had intended to push him away, but realized immediately that her action had been a mistake. Her fingers itched to explore the muscles that flexed beneath her palms.

She lifted her face and any thought of pushing him away was arrested by the look in his eyes.

Ian was stunned by the sensations created from simply holding her in his arms. When he looked into her eyes, he could no longer resist the temptation he had been fighting for weeks.

He lowered his head slowly, as if giving her time to call a halt to his purpose. Zoe had no intention of stopping him. As his mouth came down on hers, her eyes closed once more and her arms came up to encircle his neck. His lips danced lightly over hers, tasting and teasing. Her soft lips tasted so sweet, with a hint of the lemonade she had been drinking earlier. The scent of gardenias wafted up to his nostrils, as his arms tightened around her. With her breasts crushed to his chest, he could feel her nipples through the soft fabric of her dress and his thin shirt.

Zoe moaned when his tongue searched the moist recesses of her mouth. At first he was content to stroke her back through the thin fabric. But that was simply not enough, and soon his hand came up to stroke the bare, silky skin between her shoulder blades. She shivered in response, and Ian realized they were both on the brink of entering dangerous territory.

He loosened his hold slightly and lifted his head, after one last, brief kiss. Zoe opened her eyes and met his gaze. The desire she had recognized earlier was still burning in his eyes. Its intensity and her own responses warned her of the danger of her emotions.

She unwound her arms from his neck and dropped her hands to rest in her lap. Ian released her from his embrace and stood up. Their gazes held, but for a long moment, neither of them uttered a word. Zoe was the first to speak, finding it necessary to clear her throat to force the words out.

"I guess I'd better see what's in there to fix for dinner," she murmured, standing up.

"Zoe, don't you think we should discuss what's happening?"

"Nothing's happening, Ian. I think this was a normal reaction to the situation. I was upset and you were trying to comfort me," she insisted.

"Besides," she added, "one kiss doesn't require a long involved explanation or dissection." Her attempt to sound nonchalant was not very successful.

"I see," he replied, retreating a few steps to give her more space.

As she brushed past him, his final words did not escape her. "I think you're deceiving yourself. However, if you really do believe that, I suggest you prepare yourself for a surprising revelation."

For days after that disturbing encounter, Zoe kept her distance from Ian. She avoided him as much as possible. Considering the fact that they were alone on a small island, some contact with him was inevitable. She usually saw him briefly at breakfast, and they still shared the evening meal, but their conversation never touched on the emotions that lay just beneath the surface.

Although she refused to discuss these feelings, she could not ignore them. Until now she had always felt in control of her emotions. Her past experience with men was limited, but she had not lived the life of a recluse. The truth was, none of them had aroused much of an emotional response.

Even the one intimate encounter she had in college had occurred more as a result of curiosity than any great passion. After that she had never cared deeply enough for anyone to consider repeating the experience. None of the men she had dated had prepared her for her reactions to Ian.

She had felt the difference from the very beginning. She had certainly never responded to anyone as intensely as she had to him. One little kiss had told her that much. Of course, one could hardly call the kiss they had shared "little."

Her loss of memory was a large part of her reason for restraint. She knew nothing about him except what he had told her, and that was not much. Considering the circumstances under which he had revealed that slight information, she had no reason to question the truth of his statements. The problem was, it told her very little about him.

If she could remember more about herself, she would at least know why she had been aboard his yacht. What did she do for a living? That piece of information might explain her presence there. That, in turn, should give her a better clue as to who he was.

She had racked her brain time and time again, trying to recall some small bit of information. All she had gotten for her efforts was a headache. The only clue she had was her first name, and that had come out of the blue. While the recollections of her inability to swim and her allergy to shellfish were undoubtedly important, they were useless in terms of revealing her identity.

So, in addition to the amnesia, she was faced with another dilemma. She was already physically attracted to and rapidly becoming emotionally entangled with a man who, for all intents and purposes, was a total stranger. If she were not experiencing it for herself, she would have said it was impossible. How could you fall in love with someone you barely knew?

There, she had actually admitted the truth. All her thoughts about physical attraction and desire had simply been skirting the real issue. She was falling in love with Ian Roberts.


Ian was aware that Zoe was deliberately avoiding him. He had considered pressing the issue, but he discarded that idea almost immediately. With what he had learned about her personality, it was likely that such an action would only push her farther away. He also admitted that considering their circumstances, he had no right to try to persuade her into an intimate relationship.

He was surprised at the intensity of his own responses. If it could be explained as simple physical desire, he might have been able to overlook it. What defied comprehension were the feelings of tenderness and protectiveness for a woman about whom he knew next to nothing.

He had almost convinced himself that there had to be a reason for her being aboard the *Queen Bea,* other than the obvious one. He recognized that this conclusion was probably mostly wishful thinking on his part.

If his suspicions about her proved to be correct, he could not afford to allow his emotions to become involved. For days, he had been considering the danger in this development. He had finally, and somewhat reluctantly, concluded that reasoning and logic had no bearing on the matter. His feelings could not be controlled.

He had learned that the hard way when he had given in to temptation and kissed her. She had brushed it off as his attempt to comfort her. He would like to believe that had been the uppermost thought in his mind at the time, but he had been fighting the physical attraction from the first time he saw her.

The kiss had told him exactly how much he wanted her. It had also opened a Pandora's box, for both of them. The most he could do was to control his reactions to the feelings she aroused.

He had hoped that the land was where he had given
it to someone, and loved her. She had floated it off
a struggle to position her. He would like to believe that
had been the oppression thought in his mind at the time,
but he had been making the practical transition from the
first time he saw her.

The Mrs. had sent him exactly how much he wanted her.
It had also noticed window's now, the look of motel the
now the still do was required threat than to the boat had
she around.

# CHAPTER TWELVE

For the next two weeks, their mutual avoidance continued. Ian spent most of his time in his study. Zoe's days
were filled with walks on the beach, or sitting in the gazebo
reading. More often than not, however, she found herself
staring out at the ocean. Although he was making headway
with his plans, Ian spent an inordinate amount of time
thinking about her.

He marveled again at her ability to make the best of her
predicament. Although it had been his own suggestion
that she think of her time on the island as a vacation, he
was a little surprised at how much pleasure she seemed to
derive from her surroundings. He tried to put himself in
her place. How would he feel, having no clue to his identity? Having to go on week after week and month after
month with his past a total blank.

He considered all of the facets that made up one's identity. It was more than just a name. It was family and friends,
one's occupation, hobbies and pastimes. All these things
and so much more.

As his thoughts traveled along these lines, he recalled

the request he had made to his brother. He pulled out his cell phone and called Derek. They chatted for a while, Ian inquiring after the family and the company. Derek assured him that all was well.

"How are you coming along?"

"I'm almost finished. I expect I'll be ready to meet with you and Jared again within the next two weeks. I'll give you a call next week and set up a date and time. That's not the reason I called, though.

"Since you haven't called me, I assume Jared hasn't had any luck in coming up with Zoe's identity?"

"Nothing specific, but he thinks he has a good lead. He may know something by the time we meet with you. Has she remembered anything else?"

Ian thought about her recollection of her allergy, and what that recollection had prompted. "Nothing of importance."

Derek was baffled. "Oh. I thought maybe you were calling because you had more clues."

"No, unfortunately there's no progress in that area. I just thought I'd touch base with you to see if Jared had come up with any more information. I'm getting a little concerned about the possibility of her facing eviction. Take care of that matter of the rent as soon as you have her address. Considering the time that's passed, it may already be a problem."

"I'll take care of it. Don't worry about it too much, though, Ian. Even if the landlord has started legal proceedings it would take a while for the actual eviction."

"You're right. At least that's in our favor. I'm sure he'll be content just to get his rent."

"I'll let you know if I get any more information before we meet."

Ian put away the telephone, stood up, and stretched. He left the study and went to the kitchen for a drink. At least that was what he told himself. On his way back to the study, he stopped for a moment. Looking out the living room window, he watched Zoe walking on the beach. He went over in his mind the conversation he had just had with his brother. Hopefully, Derek would have the information he needed before any formal notice was given or action taken.

Maybe guaranteeing that she would not return to find her life in a state of financial ruin could assuage his conscience. In spite of his suspicions, he did occasionally have moments of doubt concerning his action.

He also had more than an occasional moment of intense attraction to his reluctant guest. He had convinced himself that it was only a minor problem, until he had kissed her. He had been unable to erase that kiss from his mind. It had almost been his undoing.

It occurred to him that if he could tell Derek about these feelings, it would certainly quell any idea his brother had that he still harbored feelings for Sharmane. On the other hand, it would make his brother more determined than ever that she should be returned to the mainland. No, his feelings for Zoe could not be revealed to his brother, not until he knew more about her. Depending upon what happened when this was all over, he might never be able to reveal his feelings.

He watched Zoe come up the walkway and stroll over to the gazebo. The graceful sway of her hips captivated him. He noticed, for the first time, that her hair was longer than it had been when she first arrived on the island.

It had been a mop of loose curls then, barely reaching her neck. Now the curls were almost to her shoulders. Either hairstyle was becoming to her. At the moment, he felt that anything would be becoming to her.

Recognizing the danger in the direction his thoughts had taken, he moved away from the window and returned to the study and the work on his desk. In another week he would be ready to put the second part of his plan into action.

# CHAPTER THIRTEEN

As he had promised, the following week Ian called his brother. They arranged to meet in Savannah on Saturday.

Ian knew Zoe would be upset when she learned he was planning another trip to the mainland. Since they were barely speaking, anyway, he might as well wait until just before he was ready to leave.

His guilt drove him to put up his own barriers between them. If Zoe'd had a change of heart and felt inclined to talk, he gave her no opportunity. He had even returned to his original habit of eating dinner in his study.

Zoe was puzzled by his action. After all, it was not as though they had argued. She conceded that she had probably contributed to his withdrawal from her. She had thought that eventually they would get over the initial awkwardness. At least they had been somewhat friendly prior to the kiss. It was ironic that a kiss appeared to be responsible for driving them apart.

It occurred to her that she should be grateful for the change. She was becoming too attached to him for her own good. The longer she stayed isolated with him on this island, the greater the danger to her emotional state.

Saturday morning Ian prepared himself for Zoe's anger at being left behind, again. He had not anticipated the possibility that her reaction would be anything but anger.

He had eaten breakfast and was having a final cup of coffee when she entered the kitchen. They murmured their greetings; in spite of everything, the niceties of everyday manners had not been forgotten. He joined her at the counter as she poured a cup of coffee.

"I'll be leaving for the mainland in a few minutes. I'll be back later this afternoon."

The look she gave him made Ian feel two inches tall. Taking her mug, she turned away from him and went to sit at the table he had vacated.

With her eyes focused on the scene outside the glass doors directly across from her, she murmured, "I won't ask you to take me with you. Obviously, you have no such plans and I refuse to beg."

If the look she had given him earlier had stabbed him in the heart, her words turned the knife. He opened his mouth to answer, but stopped. There was nothing he could say.

Zoe stayed rooted to the spot as he left the room. Moments later, she watched through the doors as he made his way to the pier. A tear trickled down her cheek as she watched the yacht pull away and head toward Savannah.

Ian pulled into the slip and turned off the motor. He had tried to put Zoe out of his mind, but her last words kept echoing in his head. He had a job to do. He could not allow himself to forget that she might be a very real danger to achieving his goal if she regained her memory before their plans reached fruition.

Derek was waiting for him dockside. They had arranged to meet Jared at a hotel. It would afford them much more privacy to finalize their plans. As Derek drove through the city, it occurred to him that it might be best to discuss Ian's earlier request before they joined their friend.

"Jared has come up with a likely identity for Zoe. Of course, we couldn't be one hundred percent sure, but he checked out all of the information thoroughly and there was very little room for doubt.

"I went to the address he gave me and the fact that the landlord hadn't seen her for a while and her rent was in arrears, pretty much confirmed it. I took care of your request. I don't know if the landlord bought my explanation, or if he was just happy to get his rent money."

"What did you tell him?"

"That she had been in an accident, that I was her brother and I wanted to take care of everything so she wouldn't have to worry about it when she came out of the hospital. I considered trying to get him to let me into her apartment, but it occurred to me that he would find it strange that she hadn't given me her key."

"I'm glad you thought about that. You might have blown everything otherwise. I do appreciate your help, Derek."

His brother wondered if he would still appreciate it when he learned the identity of his guest. He had already decided that he would leave that revelation to Jared.

A short time later the three men were settled in the hotel room. They ordered lunch from room service and Jared proceeded to fill Ian in on his discoveries.

"As you know, I've been tailing your suspect. For someone involved in something this big, he doesn't appear to be too bright. The fact that Derek caught him in a suspicious situation should have detered him in the very beginning."

"I suspect he was the one who stole one of our games last year. If that's the case, I suppose he decided he was ready for bigger and better things.

"You would think, though, that he would have enough

sense to reconsider his plans when Derek saw him coming from my office. The excuse he gave was obviously weak.

"And later, when he went through my desk, he should have at least made certain he had left everything in order. I guess he just thinks he's so smart, he has us fooled.

"The truth is, even from the beginning, I never quite trusted him. His interest in all the new software designs, whether he was directly involved with them or not, always seemed strange. It was a little more than I would have expected from an employee."

"I don't think he ever really thought of himself as just an employee," Derek reminded him. "I think he believed the fact that his mother is a friend of Mom's, gave him an edge."

"Well," Ian indicated, "his egotism will work in our favor. It will never occur to him that the software and designs were planted specifically for him to find."

Jared listened to this exchange and shook his head. "It amazes me that he would think he could outsmart you, considering what it is he's trying to steal. I suppose he thought you were a computer nerd who was totally removed from everything around him.

"I have to admit that when you told me that you had designed the solution to the problem of converting dates in preparation for the millennium, I was floored. I've seen too many examples of your intelligence to doubt you, but I still find it hard to believe."

He looked at Ian. "It really works?"

"Oh, it works," his friend assured him. "It will read the numbers in files, as well their context. It will recognize dates and change them to eight-digit, rather than six-digit numbers, giving the whole number for the year. In addition to this, and even more important than changing the dates on the files, it will identify the date on the chip and rewrite the output as an eight digit number."

They were interrupted by a knock on the door. Their lunch had arrived and the next few minutes were spent sorting it out and settling down to eat. A few minutes later, Ian turned to Jared.

"So, what did you learn from following Chad?"

"I found out that his direct contact is a man named Burnett. Burnett owns a store that sells computers, peripherals, software, and such. However, all indications are that the store is just a front. My less reputable contacts tell me he also deals in stolen goods, although he's somehow managed to stay one step ahead of the police.

"I spoke to a friend of mine, a sergeant in the police department, who told me that they've recently had some suspicions about him, but not enough to act. When I explained what we suspected and what we have in mind, he agreed to help. They'll be ready when it's time to spring the trap."

"I think that should be in about a week, maybe ten days," Ian surmised.

"Once Derek plants the package, it's not likely he'll wait long to get his hands on it. We'll only have to wait until he arranges the sale."

"You know, Ian, from what I've learned of Burnett, I'm sure that this big a deal is out of his league. He has to be acting as a middleman for someone with really big bucks. I haven't been able to find out the name of his buyer, but, for our purposes that's not important."

Ian retrieved a package from his briefcase and handed it to Derek. "This is the real software. It's all set to go."

"Wait at least a week, though. The other package will be safely in the copyright office by then, not that it really matters."

"What do you mean?" Jared asked. "It could matter a great deal if something goes wrong with our plans and he actually gets away with the software."

"What he's trying to tell you, Jared, is that the bait is a fake."

"So, what happens when he tests it. Whoever the buyer

is, you can be sure he'll check it out before he lays out any money."

Ian smiled. "Oh, it will work."

Jared shook his head. "I'm missing something."

"It's booby-trapped, Jared."

"Is that a good idea? If he does get away with it somehow, what will it do to the records of the company that buys it? After all, they'll be buying it in good faith, with no idea that it's been stolen. It might even involve government agencies, and that could really be a mess."

"Calm down, Jared. It's not that kind of booby trap. Designing that part of the software is what's given me the biggest problem. I had to be sure it wouldn't cause the kind of disaster you mentioned.

"The software will work when tested and it will work when installed. However, there's an added piece to the fake software, but it won't actually destroy anything. On a specific date, approximately ninety days from today, the software will change all of the dates back to their original numbers.

"After it does that, and just before it self-destructs, it will run a message informing the user that it was stolen. It will also tell the user the name of the designer."

Jared laughed. "You're kidding! You can actually do something like that?"

Ian shook his head. "Jared, you're a great detective, but when this is all over, Derek and I are going to have to work on your computer education."

Derek chuckled. "Not me, big brother. I've already taken a stab at that. He insists that since his wife handles the paperwork and is quite knowledeable, he doesn't need to learn any more than he already knows. Doris says he's hopeless, and I'm beginning to agree. You'll be on your own with those computer lessons."

The three friends finalized their plans while they finished their meal. Derek would contact Ian as soon as they decided when to plant the fake software for Chad to find.

"As I said, we'll assume that he'll meet with Burnett as soon as he has the software. I'm sure, other than the fact that he'll want his money, he won't want to hang on to it any longer than necessary. He would have to know that everyone in the company will be suspect as soon as we discover that it's missing."

Ian was returning some files to his briefcase, preparing to leave, when Jared dropped his bombshell. "I almost forgot one important piece of information. The woman that was on your yacht is Zoe Johnson. She works for Burnett. She's his store manager."

Ian's hand froze in midair. He took a deep breath before asking, "Are you sure?"

"I'm afraid so. I made some discrete inquiries at Burnett's store. When I asked to speak with the manager, I was told that the former manager had left and a new one hadn't been hired. The clerk said that the former manager, Zoe Johnson, had left about two months ago, supposedly to return to teaching."

"She's a school teacher?"

"Evidently. The clerk I spoke with knew very little, other than the fact that she simply failed to show up one day. When she didn't show up, the other employees were later informed by Burnett that she had quit. The clerk knew that Zoe had been a teacher and assumed that was her reason for leaving. I didn't want to probe too deeply and have her start wondering why I was so curious."

"I see."

Derek watched his brother closely during this exchange. The expression on Ian's face confirmed his suspicions. "I'm sorry, Ian," he murmured.

Ian shrugged. "Don't worry about it, Derek. I can't say it comes as a complete surprise. After all, I was the one who suspected her from the beginning, remember."

"I remember," Derek agreed. Avoiding his brother's gaze, he asked, "So where does that leave us, concerning our plans?"

"It doesn't change our plans," he said, closing his brief-case with a snap. He looked up at Derek.

"If you don't mind, I need to do a little shopping before I head back to the island." Obviously, the discussion about Zoe was closed.


The car pulled up to the curb slowly. The young man stepped out of the vehicle and looked around furtively. He never liked leaving his BMW parked in this part of town. Why did Burnett insist on meeting here anyway?

The car and the expensive suit he wore were out of place in these surroundings. But then, the car and expensive suit were two of the reasons for his being there. He had expensive tastes and this was the only way to pay for the good life. His salary just never seemed to be enough.

He entered the warehouse by the side entrance and went straight to the cubbyhole Burnett referred to as an office. He looked around at the stacks of cartons containing merchandise that he had no doubt was stolen.

Burnett was waiting, not very patiently. The "office" was filled with cigar smoke. Hopefully, this meeting would be brief.

"It's about time, Gordon. Have you made any progress?"

"I expect to have the merchandise within a few weeks."

"That's what you said a month ago."

"I don't have any control over when the product will be finished. I told you he left town, but from what I've heard, the software should be completed soon."

"Are you sure you'll be able to get your hands on it?"

"I told you I've done this before. Have you had any luck finding the woman?"

Burnett shook his head. "She's disappeared. I knew she'd never return to the store. I had one of my men watching her apartment for a while. She never showed up there, either."

"You don't sound concerned about it."

"I'm not. What can she do? She couldn't have overheard enough to be any danger to us. She doesn't know you. Even if she went to the police, what could she tell them? I'd have heard from them by now, if she had given them anything to go on."

Chad had given the impression that he was confident about succeeding. What he did not tell the other man was that he had had a close call recently. He was seen coming out of the boss's office. He had not taken anything, so his explanation for being there had been accepted.

The game he had stolen the previous year was small-time compared to what he was after now. He would be set for years, maybe for life, with what he expected to make from this sale.

Recalling that previous transaction, he wondered who Burnett had found that could afford a purchase of this magnitude.

"Who's the buyer?"

Burnett's eyes narrowed. "You don't need to know that. All you need to know is that he can afford to pay the price. You'll get your money."

Chad shrugged. He did not really care what happened to the software once he had his money. He did resent the fact that he had to use Burnett as a middleman. He could have made ten times as much on the sale if he had the contacts to find a buyer with that kind of money. Maybe that was why Burnett was so closemouthed about it.

"Fine with me. I'll call you when I have the merchandise in my hand."

Burnett watched him go. He did not trust him. Not that he thought he would be stupid enough to try to double-cross him, he just had doubts about his ability to pull off this kind of deal.

# CHAPTER FOURTEEN

Zoe sat at the kitchen table for a long time after Ian left. She had not really expected him to take her with him. If he would only tell her why he refused to let her leave, it might be a little easier to accept—although she could not imagine any acceptable excuse for his actions.

Unless he knew more about her than he admitted. Maybe he actually knew her. That would make sense, except it would also mean that she knew him. It was hard to believe she could actually know him and have no recollection of it, especially having spent all these weeks alone with him. On the other hand, if he was a total stranger, what would she have been doing on his boat?

She knew she was grasping at straws. It was hard to believe that his sympathy at the loss of her memory had been feigned. Besides, he had seemed to be interested in helping her, taking her aboard the yacht in an attempt to jog her memory. If he had been withholding information about her, would he have told her so much about his own family? If she was acquainted with them, it might have given her some clue to her own identity. Zoe sighed.

*You know what the real problem is, girlfriend? You're falling for the man and the longer you stay here the more entangled your feelings will become.*

She recalled his tenderness when she had been upset about the bird and his concern when she told him about her allergy to shellfish. That thought led to the recollection of his kiss.

Her thoughts chased around in her head until she was thoroughly confused. She dressed and went outside. Wandering aimlessly up and down the beach did not clear her head, as she had hoped. The only conclusion she reached was that she was falling in love with Ian Roberts, which she already knew.

She again considered the possibility that he actually knew her. Surely, if that were the case, he would have given her some clues to try to help her regain her memory. He had seen how upset she was. Why would he let her go through this distress if he had information that could help her? Unless he had reasons not to want her to remember.

The more she thought about it, the closer she came to the obvious solution. She had to put some distance between them; physical distance, not just her meager attempts to ignore him.

As she walked the beach for the tenth time, she looked over at the pier. The only boat still moored there was a small motorboat. She had seen it before, on her other explorations of the yacht. It now occurred to her that this one looked small enough for her to handle.

A thought formed in her head. Surely there would be a compass on board. She was no boater, but how hard could it be?

She thought she recalled Derek mentioning that they were only five miles from the mainland. All she had to do was keep the boat headed due west and she would be bound to reach land. Even if she did not reach Savannah, any town would serve the purpose. She would simply go to the authorities and explain her situation.

Ian was convinced that she had no choice but to wait for him to release her. It would serve him right to return and find her, and his boat, gone.

Without any more thought about what she was attempting, she hurried over to the boat and climbed in. The key was in the ignition, one problem solved. There was a compass, second problem overcome. Shakily she slipped the rope from the moorings, started the engine, and steered away from the pier.

Just when she was beginning to think her plan would actually work, the engine began to sputter. Moments later, it stopped. She tried the ignition again, but nothing happened. She tried several more times with no luck. She was stuck in the middle of the ocean. All she could do was wait and pray that someone came along.

Two hours after their meeting, Derek dropped his brother off at the pier. He had briefly brought Ian up to date on the company business, although he was not sure just how much of his information fell on deaf ears. His brother was obviously, and understandably, proccupied. No further references were made to their stowaway.

"Call me as soon as you have everything set up."

They said their good-byes and Derek watched him walk down the pier. He waited until Ian had manuevered the yacht from the slip and was on his way back to the island, before driving away. All the signs were there. He knew his brother well and, unless he was totally off the mark for the first time since they had reached adulthood, Ian was on his way to falling in love.

Ian suspected his reaction to the news of Zoe's identity had given Derek a clue to his predicament. He was not yet ready to admit his feelings to his brother, but he would not lie to himself. The strength of his feelings could no longer be denied, although he still hesitated to call it love.

As he steered the boat he could not help thinking about

the woman waiting for him. He ignored the fact that she
was not waiting willingly.

In spite of the evidence Jared had presented, he had
difficulty believing she was involved in anything illegal. He
told himself that just because she was involved in Burnett's
legitimate business did not mean she was a participant in
the illegal activities. The unwelcome little voice in his head
reminded him that the fact that she had been hiding on
the *Queen Bea* was reason enough to suggest she was implicated in the crime.

In any event, whatever her part had been up to this time,
she would not be in on any of their future plans. When
the time came to set the trap, she would be on the island.
He could not ignore the possibility that she might be
incriminated by the other two when they were caught.

He hoped that her absence when the others were
arrested would make it impossible to prove anything
against her. As for his personal feelings, it no longer mattered if she had been involved in the beginning. He could
ensure that she would have no further involvement.
Although it might be an unwise move, he was also determined to protect her from any implication in the theft, if
that was at all possible.

Ian was only a few miles north of the island when he
noticed a small boat that appeared to be adrift in the
channel to the west. He steered the *Queen Bea* slowly in
that direction, careful to avoid capsizing the smaller vessel
in his rescue efforts.

At first he thought a tender from another yacht had
somehow been loosened and set afloat without the owner's
knowledge. As he neared the small craft, he could see that
it had not been loosened by accident. It was occupied.

He shook his head in disbelief at the ignorance of some
boaters. Trying to navigate this channel in a boat that small
was foolhardy, to say the least.

When he was close enough to recognize the vessel as
the tender from his own yacht, his irritation turned to

anger—and fear. The occupant could only be one person—Zoe. How could she be so reckless? Aside from the obvious danger, she had already told him she was not a swimmer. She knew nothing about boating and, from what he could see, was not even wearing a life jacket.

He manuevered the *Queen Bea* until he was alongside the small craft. After shutting off the motor, he dropped the anchor and left the bridge to assess the situation.

Zoe breathed a sigh of relief when she realized she was close to being rescued. Her relief turned to dismay, however, when she recognized the vessel headed her way. When the yacht stopped alongside, she steeled herself for Ian's anger.

After dropping the anchor, he appeared at the railing. He was surprisingly calm as he lowered a ladder down the side of the *Queen Bea*. Zoe was riveted to her seat. She waited for him to climb down. Instead, he stood at the railing and issued his instructions.

"The first order of business is for you to look under the seat and get a life jacket."

"A life jacket?"

"It's just a precaution. The ladder is perfectly safe."

After she had donned the life jacket, he threw a rope down to her. She tied it to the tender as he directed and sat down to wait while he secured it to the yacht. She was totally unprepared for his next order.

"Grab the ladder and climb up, Zoe," he said, reaching down toward her with one hand.

She looked at the ladder and back at him, shaking her head.

"I don't think I can."

He would not give in to the apprehension in her eyes. "You can do it, Zoe. You only have to come up a few rungs to reach my hand. You can climb the ladder."

She slid across the seat, close enough to touch the side

of the yacht. Then she reached out and took hold of the ladder. As she placed one foot on the closest rung, her other foot pushed against the small craft causing it to drift away so that it was no longer directly beneath her. She tried to ignore the fact that she was dangling above the water.

"That's it, I knew you could do it. Considering that you were so determined to get off the island that you'd come all the way out here in that little boat, a minor feat like climbing a ladder is a piece of cake."

His words were meant to offer encouragement. Instead, it recalled her earlier anger at being left behind. She lost her concentration and slipped, falling into the water and narrowly missing the smaller boat. She gasped as she hit the water and floundered for a few seconds before it occurred to her that the life jacket would keep her afloat.

She forced herself to relax and, a moment later, Ian descended the ladder far enough to throw her a life preserver and pull her close enough for him to reach her hand. Placing her hand on the ladder, he lowered himself into the water, urging her up the ladder ahead of him. Within minutes they were both on board. Ian urged her below, to the salon and into a chair. After wrapping a blanket around her shoulders, he went to retrieve the tender.

They soon reached the island and Zoe was on the bridge the minute he docked. He had not said a word after the rescue. From the look on his face, to say he was not pleased was a gross understatement.

She had hoped to have a little time to prepare herself before the inevitable confrontation and attempted to slip past him while he was busy docking. Ian had just eased the last rope onto its mooring when she walked past him. He grabbed her arm, preventing her from making her escape.

"What possessed you to go out into those waters in a fourteen-foot tender. Even if the gas tank had been full, it's

questionable that you would have made it to the mainland.
You're lucky I returned before you drifted out of the
channel."

"If it hadn't been you, someone else would have eventually come by."

Ian shook his head. "I don't think so. Have you looked
at the sky? There's a storm coming."

He gestured to the darkening skies to the north. He
had heard about the approaching storm before leaving
Savannah, but his conscience would not allow him to leave
her alone on the island during a storm. He had gauged
the time it would take to reach the island and felt confident
he could make it before the storm hit.

The fear that sprang to her eyes told him that he had
made the right decision. It also surprised him. It had taken
no small amount of courage to set out across the channel
in a small craft with no boating skills or swimming ability.
But now, she appeared terrified by the approach of a simple
thunderstorm.

There was a tremor in her voice when she asked, "Is it
a hurricane?"

That was why she was so frightened, he thought. "No,
Zoe. It's just a thunderstorm."

The fear in her eyes did not subside. "How can you be
sure?"

"It's not hurricane season, yet. You must be aware that
they only come at certain times of the year," he assured
her.

She shivered. Her fear of the storm had made her forget
that she was soaked to the skin.

"You'd better go and get out of those clothes."

Zoe needed no further encouragement. She turned and
hurried along the pier and up the beach. Heedless of his
own wet clothing, Ian watched her for a moment before
returning to the task of preparing the yacht for the coming
storm.

Months ago, when he had found her trying to use the

radio, it had occurred to him that she might try to take Derek's cabin cruiser. Since then he had convinced himself that she would never attempt to leave the island on her own. He certainly did not expect that she would attempt it in a fourteen-foot tender.

When he saw her out there in the channel, his first reaction had been anger at her rashness. That emotion had soon changed to fear. There was no telling what could have happened to her if he had returned an hour or two later. It was very likely that the small boat would have drifted beyond his sight or, even worse, capsized.

Aside from the anger and fear, he also felt guilty for being responsible for her being in such a desperate situation. After all this time, he could not imagine why she had suddenly decided she had to get off the island at all costs.

He refused to entertain the notion that she had regained her memory and was trying to get back to her cohorts. If she had, indeed, recovered from her amnesia, she would likely give herself away before long.

Seeing her in such immediate danger had also made him realize exactly how much she meant to him. If anything happened to her, whether it was his fault or not, he was not sure he would get over it.

If what he felt was not love, it was dangerously close to the real thing—he had not realized just how close, until that moment. He realized something else, too. He would do everything he could to protect her, in spite of the information he had received from Jared earlier that day.

When he entered the house, Ian was surprised that she was nowhere in sight. He had no doubt that she was angry with him. It also occurred to him that she was probably hungry. He had no idea how long she had been adrift, but it was now well past dinner time. He knew enough about her temperament to think that she might never come out of her room if it meant facing him.

When he knocked on her door, he received no reply. He was determined not to let her shut him out again. He could not have said what he expected to find when he opened the door, but the bedroom was empty. With her obvious terror of the coming storm, it was extremely doubtful that she had gone out of the house.

He was puzzled for a moment, until he heard the shower. He turned to leave and stopped dead in his tracks. Zoe had stepped out of the shower and with the bathroom door open, her glistening body was reflected in the mirror directly across from him. He was transfixed by the vision of her silky skin and enticingly rounded bottom.

She turned to reach for the towel, unwittingly exposing to his view the full breasts he had only glimpsed before, as well as the other treasures he had only imagined. Ian drew in his breath and fought to control his body's reaction. He finally managed to break himself from his trance when she wrapped the towel around her body, unknowingly shielding it from his view. Ian retreated quickly and quietly from the room.

When Zoe entered the kitchen half an hour later, Ian had changed out of his wet clothes and was busy at the stove. Without uttering a word to him, she walked directly to the sliding glass doors, looking out at the rain that had started falling a few minutes earlier. Moments later a clap of thunder sounded overhead, accompanied by a flash of lightning. She flinched and quickly retreated to the table.

"I realize that the isolation here makes window coverings unnecessary, but you really should consider hanging drapes or blinds."

If he had not seen the genuine fear in her eyes earlier that day, Ian would have been amused at her suggestion. He looked across the room to where she sat at the table, her back to the doors.

She was wearing a modest, loose-fitting sundress in a

brightly colored flowered print of reds and golds. In his mind's eye, Ian saw, not the colorful garment, but the lush curves of her naked body.

When she looked up, their eyes met. Zoe's mouth went suddenly dry. The look in his eyes was very different from the anger she had seen there when he rescued her. She might not be experienced with men, but she recognized desire when she saw it and it was not the first time she had seen it in his eyes. She had to admit, though, it had never been quite as intense as it was at that moment. Neither of them seemed able to look away, until the ordinary sound of the microwave timer broke the spell. Reluctantly, Ian returned to his food preparations. It was then that he realized that she might have expected a reply to her observation on the lack of window coverings.

"You mentioned the need for blinds. I never really thought about it, except in my bedroom. On those rare days that I decide to sleep in, the sun's rays at dawn do not inspire me to action."

"Doesn't your sister mind the early morning sun when she's here?"

Ian laughed. "Not at all. She's one of those disgusting people who are always up at the crack of dawn."

As he spoke, he went to the refrigerator and brought out a large bowl. Picking up the platter of chicken from the counter, he carried them both to the table.

The entangled, confusing emotions of anger and desire, although not entirely forgotten, were set aside, at least for the moment. They settled down to their meal in silence.

Zoe enjoyed her meal for about ten minutes. That was when the storm seemed to escalate, and her appetite began to rapidly disappear. With each clap of thunder, the tension in her body increased. She finally gave up and rose from the table, taking her plate to the sink.

Her distress had not gone unnoticed. "Is that all you're eating?"

She shrugged. "I guess I wasn't as hungry as I thought."

Her task completed, she had returned to the table. She picked up her glass and almost dropped it when an especially loud clap of thunder sounded directly overhead.

"Well, I'll say good night."

"Good night? It's not even eight o'clock."

"It's been a long day and I'm exhausted. Actually, I may read for a while."

Ian hesitated. He refrained from mentioning the most likely reason for her exhaustion. She was, obviously, unwilling to acknowledge her fear of the storm. Otherwise, it would have been more logical not to want to be alone during the tempest.

"Yes," he said, nodding. "It has been a long day. Good night, then."

As she walked past him, he felt compelled to add, "Zoe, try not to worry about the storm. It's loud, but there isn't any real danger."

She nodded, but Ian could see that she did not really believe him. He watched her go, wishing there was more he could say or do to ease her apprehension. He was aware that there were many adults who experienced an unreasoning fear of thunderstorms. It surprised him that she was one of them. She had shown such courage in the face of more frightening situations.

When she reached her room, Zoe shed her clothes and slipped into her pajamas. She felt chilled, but was not certain if it was because the temperature had dropped or if it was simply a result of her fear. She added a robe over the pajamas and pulled an extra blanket from the closet. If she could only remember why she was afraid of storms, it might be easier to cope with it.

One reason for seeking refuge in her room had been her increased attraction to Ian. Her attempt at escape had been a resounding failure. She hoped that removing herself from his presence now would give her a chance to bring her wayward emotions under control. It might help her cope better with the storm if she eased the other cause of her tension.

Aside from that, she had hoped that she could lose herself in a book. Maybe it would help distract her from the lightning flashing outside the glass doors of the bedroom.

Unfortunately, she had chosen a murder mystery, which did nothing to ease her frame of mind. When the third body was discovered, she decided she had had enough. She set the book aside, turned out the light and snuggled down under the covers, her back to the glass doors.

# CHAPTER FIFTEEN

It was after midnight when Zoe was awakened by the storm. It seemed that this particular storm had settled over the island with no intention of moving on. She had no way of knowing that there had been a brief lull while she slept. For half an hour, she lay there vainly trying to go back to sleep. It did no good to turn her back to the glass doors; when the lightning flashed, it lit up the entire room. She finally gave up.

Ian had said that there were drapes at the window in his room. That bit of knowledge was no help. She could just imagine herself barging into his room and settling down in bed beside him. Fortunately, the distraction of the storm turned her mind from the natural progression of such ideas.

Maybe she could find another spot that was shielded from the outside. She threw back the covers and was immediately aware that the temperature had, indeed, dropped. Throwing the blanket around her shoulders, she left the room.

She searched the entire house and she did find two

other bedrooms with drapes, sheer drapes which were no help at all. As she made her way back to her room, it struck her that the hallway was the only place where the lightning flashes were not visible. She was glad he had not seen fit to add skylights to the structure. She was desperate; it sounded as though the storm would never end and she was exhausted. Maybe if she sat here for a while the storm would move on.

She wrapped the blanket more tightly around her and sat down on the floor to wait it out. Drawing her knees up to her chest, she rested her forehead on them. With any luck, she might even manage to take a short nap.

She had been sitting there for almost an hour when Ian opened his bedroom door. He could not explain what had awakened him, but once he was awake he had felt the need to check on her. He was thoroughly puzzled when he saw her huddled on the floor.

"Zoe, what are you doing out here?" he asked, approaching her.

His voice startled her. She could think of no acceptable reply to his question. When she did not respond, Ian repeated his question.

This time he received a reply, of sorts. "Nothing. I'm not doing anything."

Ian sighed and knelt down beside her. "You know what I meant. Why are you sitting out here on the floor?"

Another clap of thunder made her jump. "How long do these storms last? Are you sure it's not a hurricane?"

"To answer your first question, there were several storms, following behind each other. As to your second question, I assure you it's not hurricane season."

"Does the storm know that?"

He had come to understand that her attempt at humor usually hid a more serious emotion. He gently touched her shoulder.

"I promise you, it's not a hurricane. Is that why you're out here, because you're afraid of thunderstorms?"

This fall, BET Arabesque Films will create 10 original African American themed, made-for-TV movies based on the Arabesque Romance book series.

The list includes some of the best-loved Arabesque romances including Francis Ray's *Incognito*, Donna Hill's *Intimate Betray* Bridget Anderson's *Rendezvous*, Lynn Emery's *After All*, Felici Mason's *Rhapsody*, Monica Jackson's *Midnight Blue*, Dianne Mayhew's *Playing with Fire*, Donna Hill's *A Private Affair*, Jacquelin Thomas' *Hidden Blessings, and* Donna Hill's *Masquerade*.

And now BET is offering you the chance to win a cameo appearance in one of these upcoming productions! Just think, you can join some of today's hottest African-American movie stars—like Richard T. Jones, Loretta Devine, and Holly Robinson—in the creation of a movie written by, and for, African-American romantics like yourself! All you have to do is complete the attached entry form and mail it in. Just think, if you act now, you could be in one of these exciting new movies! Mail your entry today!

## PRIZES
The **GRAND PRIZE WINNER** will receive:
- A trip for two to Los Angeles.
  Think about it—3 days and 2 nights in L.A., round-trip airfare, hotel accommodations.

- $500 spending money, and round-trip transportation to and from the airport and movie set...sounds pretty good, right?

- And the winner's clip will be featured on the Arabesque website!

- As if that's not enough, you'll also get a one-year membership in the Arabesque Book Club and a BET Arabesque Romance gift-pack.

## 5 RUNNERS-UP will receive:
- One-year memberships in the Arabesque Book Club and BET Arabesque Romance gift-packs.

# WIN A CHANCE TO BE IN A BET ARABESQUE FILM!

**Yes!** Enter me in the BET Arabesque Film Sweepstakes!

NAME _____

ADDRESS _____

CITY _____ STATE _____ ZIP _____

TELEPHONE _____

SIGNATURE _____ AGE _____

(MUST BE 21 OR OLDER TO ENTER)

Visit our website at www.arabesquebooks.com

ARABESQUE FILM SWEEPSTAKES
P.O. BOX 8060
GRAND RAPIDS, MN 55745-8060

# An important message from the ARABESQUE Editor

Dear Arabesque Reader,

Because you've chosen to read one of our Arabesque romance novels, we'd like to say "thank you"! And, as a special way to thank you, we've selected four more of the books you love so well to send you absolutely FREE!

Please enjoy them with our compliments, and thank you for continuing to enjoy Arabesque...the soul of romance.

*Karen R. Thomas*

Karen Thomas
Senior Editor,
Arabesque Romance Novels

# 3 QUICK STEPS
# TO RECEIVE YOUR FREE "THANK YOU" GIFT
# FROM THE EDITOR

Send back this card and you'll receive 4 Arabesque novels—
absolutely free!  These books have a combined cover price of
$20.00 or more, but they are yours to keep absolutely free.

There's no catch.  You're under no obligation to buy anything.
We charge nothing for the books—ZERO—for your 4 free
books (except $1.50 for shipping and handling).  And you
don't have to make any minimum number of purchases—
not even one!

We hope that after receiving your free books you'll want to
remain an Arabesque subscriber.  But the choice is yours to
continue or cancel, anytime at all!  So why not take us up on
our invitation to receive your free gift, with no risk of any
kind.  You'll be glad you did!

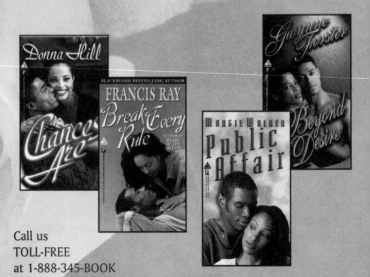

Call us
TOLL-FREE
at 1-888-345-BOOK

"I'm not afraid. I just don't like them."

He took a deep breath. "Zoe, people don't sit in dark hallways in the middle of the night simply because they dislike storms."

Until that moment, she had avoided looking at him. Now, she glared at him, but did not respond. She would not admit such a childish fear to him.

"Be reasonable, Zoe, you can't sit out here in the hallway all night. The temperature has dropped and I'm sure you can't be very comfortable, especially hunched over like that."

"I'll be fine," she insisted.

Ian gave up trying to talk to her. He stood up and went back to his room. He returned shortly, dragging a large armchair which he pushed up against the wall next to her.

"Will you, at least, get up off the floor and sit in the chair?"

Zoe looked up at him and then at the chair. She made an attempt to stand, but her foot had gone to sleep and she had difficulty making her legs work. Ian reached down and helped her. His arms came around her, to steady her, and he found he did not want to let her go. Instead of moving aside to let her sit in the chair, he lifted her in his arms and sat down with her on his lap.

Zoe put up a feeble protest. It felt good being held in his arms. It had not registered in her mind that he was wearing only the bottom half of pajamas until she felt his bare chest against her cheek. The sensation reawakened the feelings that had been responsible for her retreat earlier that evening.

"I thought you offered me the chair."

A smile lit Ian's face as he tucked the blanket more snugly around her. "I changed my mind. I'd rather share it."

His arms tightened around her. "Try to go back to sleep."

Surprisingly, she did just that. Within half an hour, her

shallow, even breathing suggested to him that she had
fallen asleep. He stood up and carried her to her room.
He had no sooner pulled the covers up over her than
she jerked at the sound of another clap of thunder and
lightning which lit up the room.

He hesitated a moment before lifting her in his arms
and carrying her across the hall to his room. If he left her
in her own room chances were that, come morning, he
would find her folded uncomfortably in the chair in the
hall.

There was nothing he could do about the thunder, but
at least the lightning would be shut out by the drapes. He
laid her in the bed and drew the covers up. It occurred
to him that he had wanted her in his bed for weeks,
although not under these circumstances. He resigned himself to the situation and went around to the other side of
the bed. Sensibly turning his back to her sleeping form,
he drifted off to sleep.

Ian was awakened hours later by a hand caressing his
chest. At some time during his sleep, he had rolled onto
his back. He opened his eyes and looked at Zoe, her head
resting on his shoulder and her body lying half atop his.
She was still asleep, totally unaware of what she was doing.
She was enfolded in his arm, his hand resting on her hip,
absently kneading the rounded flesh of her bottom. Ian
was very much aware of the effect their actions were having
on his body.

He stilled his hand and attempted to put some distance
between them. He soon realized that her legs were draped
across, and entangled with his. The more he moved, the
more entangled they became, until he could no longer
stand it. He was fully aroused and her hand was beginning
to stray from the relatively safe area of his upper body.

He murmured her name twice before she opened her
eyes. His own desire was mirrored in her eyes. It was his

undoing. He turned, reversing their positions, his body trapping her beneath him. His mouth came down on hers, gently at first, and then with all the hunger he had held in check for weeks.

His tongue explored, thoroughly, the sweetness he had tasted only briefly with that first kiss. While the hand beneath her continued kneading, his other hand slid under her pajama top to capture one enticing globe. His thumb caressed the already rigid peak of her breast.

The alluring scent of lavender engulfed him as she stirred in his arms. Her hands moved over his back, and lower, caressing the tight muscles of his buttocks. When she moaned, he lifted his head, reluctantly breaking the kiss. Her eyes opened in surprise, and disappointment.

"Are you sure about this, Zoe?" he whispered.

Her arms tightened around him. She was entranced by the sensation of muscles rippling beneath her fingers.

"I want you, Ian. I'm sure."

Within seconds, he had stripped and removed her pajamas and she lay naked in his arms. His hands continued to explore and fondle her body. His mouth captured hers for a brief taste of its nectar before his lips moved to her neck, his teeth nibbling her ear.

Zoe gasped when his mouth continued its journey, moving to her breast, his tongue laving the turgid nipple. Her body was on fire and she moved beneath him, unwittingly fanning the flames of desire in both of them. His hand slid down her body, coming to rest on the curly triangle of hair that shielded what was rapidly becoming the center of her universe.

Her hands moved restlessly until one grazed his fully aroused manhood. It was Ian's turn to gasp. His fingers moved even lower, seeking, and finding, the moist flesh beneath the mat of curls. He gently stroked the sensitive nub, until Zoe thought she would burst from the sheer pleasure of it.

"Please, Ian. Please."

"I aim to do just that, sweetheart."

Easing her thighs apart, he settled his body between them. Once nestled between her silky thighs, he eased his shaft into her hot, wet sheath. He hesitated, savoring the sensation. She was so tight. Every muscle in his body tensed, fighting to retain control. This was no time to be in a hurry. It seemed he had waited a lifetime for this moment.

"Don't stop."

Cradled by her thighs, he was engulfed by her sweet smell. Zoe writhed beneath him and flinched when he moved again, filling her completely before retreating slowly.

"Easy, baby. It'll be alright. I promise," he soothed.

His mouth captured hers again as he moved in a slow, steady rhythm. Zoe soon became accustomed to the unfamiliar tightness and followed his lead. She was overwhelmed by the myriad of sensations enveloping her. His scent surrounded her. The sprinkling of hairs on his chest teased her breasts.

Her hands roamed over his body, exploring the hard muscles, as her body seemed to move of its own volition, matching the rhythm he set. She moaned, clutching his shoulders, as his mouth moved to her breast, resuming the pleasant torture he had begun earlier.

He thrust deeper and faster, until she felt as if she could stand the tension no longer. She instinctively wrapped her legs around his waist.

"Please, Ian."

"Soon, baby. Very soon."

His fingers found the sensitive nub. He barely touched it before she cried out her release. Seconds later his own cries of ecstasy echoed through the room.

Ian eased from her and rolled onto his back, taking her with him. She fell asleep almost immediately, locked in the same position that had awakened him earlier. Ian lay awake for a while, his emotions in a turmoil.

He was in love with a woman about whom he knew next

to nothing, a woman who might be involved in a conspiracy to steal his software. In spite of the questions and possibilities, it felt so right, lying there with her in his arms. It was that overriding thought that stayed in his mind when he finally succumbed to sleep.

Zoe was still wrapped in Ian's arms when she awakened the next morning. She raised herself slightly on her elbow to see his face. He was still asleep, long lashes resting against his cheeks. She could feel his heartbeat beneath her hand, its rhythm slow and steady, unlike the pounding she had felt a few hours earlier.

The first time had not been enough to satisfy the hunger and they had awakened and made love again just as dawn was breaking. She indulged herself, now, for a few minutes, just looking at him and remembering the passion.

Then she sighed and disentangled her legs, but before she could turn and get out of bed his arm pulled her closer. Startled, she looked up into eyes, incredibly, still burning with desire.

"Going somewhere?" he asked, smiling.

His one hand had been resting on her hip, but before she knew what was happening, both hands encircled her waist, lifting her to lie on top of him. The evidence of his arousal was pressed against the soft curls between her thighs. His arms held her trapped in his warm embrace, the mat of hair on his chest teasing her breasts.

Zoe started to answer his question, but found it necessary to clear her throat first. The words seemed to be stuck. His hand slid down her back, caressing her derriere, and she was having difficulty breathing.

"As a matter of fact," she managed to whisper, "I was planning to get up and take a bath."

"Hmm, a bath," he murmured, nibbling her ear. "That sounds interesting. It conjures up all kinds of possibilities."

He realized that his plans would have to be changed

when he gently moved her thigh and saw her wince. How could he have been so thoughtless? He planted a brief, gentle kiss on her mouth and rolled to the side until they lay facing each other.

"Sorry, sweetheart. You're probably right. What you need is a nice long soak in a hot tub alone, unfortunately." He smiled. "Go take your bath."

Zoe turned over, trying to untangle herself from the sheets. Ian sat up and leaned back against the pillows, watching her. She leaned over the side of the bed, as though searching for something. A few minutes later, she had retrieved her pajama top and was struggling to put it on. She had managed to get her arms in the sleeves when her attention was drawn from her task by the sound of Ian's chuckle.

She turned to face him, frowning. "What's so funny?"

"You. A few minutes ago you lay naked on top of me, to say nothing of the passion we shared a few hours ago. Now you're trying to hide?"

Zoe blushed at the truth of his statement and her memory of the passion he mentioned. She turned her back on him and continued the task of buttoning her pajama top.

"Zoe?"

When she did not respond to her name, he leaned over, his hands encircling her waist and drawing her back to the center of the bed. Zoe gasped at this unexpected action. She could feel the heat of his body against her back, even through her pajamas. His face nuzzled her neck. He had told her to go and take her bath, but he was having difficulty letting her go.

"I didn't mean to embarrass you, but you have to admit that hiding your body from me is a just a little illogical."

Zoe shrugged. "I guess you have a point. Right now, however, I'd like to take that bath."

Ian sighed and loosened his hold. Zoe scooted back to the edge of the bed. Ian inhaled deeply when she stood up. Her pajama top barely reached the top of her thighs and his mind envisioned what he could not actually see. He closed his eyes until he heard her soft footsteps cross the hall to her room. A moment later he stepped into his own shower and turned on the cold water.

Zoe lowered her body into the soothing warm water and immersed herself in the mounds of bubbles. She closed her eyes, leaned back, and relaxed.

It was inevitable that her thoughts were filled with the events of the previous night. It had been all that she had anticipated. In hindsight, she admitted that she had been anticipating it. She had seen it coming for weeks. While being honest with herself in that admission, she also had to admit that she had no regrets.

As incredible as it seemed, she was in love with him. She had no idea who she was . . . no idea why she was here on this island. And she was in love with a man about whom she knew only what he had told her. None of that seemed to matter as far as her feelings were concerned.

She could try to rationalize her lack of resistance with her fear of the storm. Their passion had easily relegated that concern to the back of her mind. The question was whether it would develop into anything more than passion.

In spite of being in love with him, or maybe because of it, she could not help but feel some anxiety concerning the situation. After all, she might not be able to control her emotions, but she was not so foolish as to think that the answers to her questions were unimportant.

Where did they go from here? Obviously, that question could not be answered until she regained her memory. Maybe she was simply burying her head in the sand, but, for now, she would not worry about the future of their relationship. All she could do was wait and see what happened when they left the island, unless her memory returned before then.

Of course, there was always the option of calling a halt to

any further physical involvement. As soon as that thought entered her head, she discarded it. Who did she think she was kidding?

She was honest enough to acknowledge the fact that her actions were not the result of being unable to resist temptation. She had never subscribed to the excuse of irresistible urges. The truth of the matter was that she was not inclined to resist them. Furthermore, she was not convinced that there was any good reason to resist them.

# CHAPTER SIXTEEN

An hour after leaving Ian's bedroom, Zoe entered the kitchen where he was already in the process of cooking breakfast. She stood in the doorway watching the flexing of muscles in his shoulders and arms as he worked at the stove. Her gaze drifted to the taut rear end she had caressed in abandon the previous night. Her body responded to the memory and she suddenly felt unusually warm.

Ian sensed her presence and turned and smiled. "Good morning. Feeling better?"

"I'm fine," she assured him, pouring herself a mug of coffee. "What made you think I wasn't feeling well?"

Ian cleared his throat and turned back to his task. "It's not that I thought you were ill. I just noticed that you seemed to be in some discomfort. Don't misunderstand me. I'm not hinting for any revelations. It's just that, from what I recall of last night, I had the impression that it's been a long time since you were intimate with a man, if ever."

"What . . . what makes you think that?" she stammered.

Ian looked up from his task. When their eyes met, Zoe regretted her question. She blushed and looked away.

"Shall we just say that it's because of the extremely snug fit."

Zoe's head swung back around. Her mouth opened to reply, but no words came out. She almost said that she might not be the one responsible for the snug fit, but she stopped herself just in time. It was not a discussion she wished to prolong. The intimacy they had shared just a few hours earlier was too new for her to feel comfortable with an in-depth conversation concerning their love-making.

While it was true that she had awakened with an unexpected tenderness, she never expected that he would be aware of it. She was rapidly learning that there was little that escaped his notice.

Avoiding any further scrutiny, she took her mug and retreated to the table. Ian made no attempt to continue the discussion. He watched as she helped herself to the muffins he had placed on the table earlier. A few minutes later he joined her, setting a plate of sausage and eggs in front of her.

"Ian, I was planning to just have coffee and muffins. If I keep eating these big breakfasts, the only clothes that will fit will be muumuus."

"I don't think you have to worry about that. They say that exercise is the key to maintaining your weight. I'm quite willing to help you get plenty of that."

Zoe almost choked on a mouthful of muffin. "I don't think that's what the health experts had in mind."

Ian smiled. "How do you know what *I* had in mind? Maybe I was referring to jogging on the beach."

"Sure you were."

He chuckled. They resumed their meal, but Ian's attention was more on her than on his food. Their lovemaking the previous night was still fresh in his mind, but the physical relationship was only a small part of his distraction.

As unbelievable as it seemed, he was in love with her. He had always scoffed at people who professed love at first sight. Although it had not occurred at first sight, the fact that he had known her less than three months hardly made his feelings more believable than if it had happened at first sight.

Although she would have been very disappointed, Zoe had half expected that he would retreat to his den after breakfast. She had no way of knowing that his work was completed and he was now waiting for Jared and Derek to arrange everything with the police and set the trap. Instead of shutting himself in his den, he suggested a walk on the beach.

Zoe had agreed readily to the walk, but she had more than a few misgivings when he proposed a dip in the ocean. She had yet to wear either of the swimsuits he had purchased. The shallow end of a pool was fine for a nonswimmer, but the ocean was a different matter. It never occurred to her that the danger involved in a little dip in the edge of the ocean was nothing compared to her jaunt the previous day.

"I think you've forgotten one very important consideration, Ian. I can't swim."

"I haven't forgotten. I'll be with you and we won't go out far."

He lifted her hand to his lips. "Please, at least give it a try. The water will feel good."

Zoe hesitated a moment and he waited patiently. She looked out at the water. It was hard to believe a violent storm had passed through hours earlier. The waves were gently rolling onto the beach. She had to admit that there was nothing threatening about their appearance.

"Alright," she replied at last, looking up at him. "I'll go and change into my suit."

Ian smiled. "That really isn't necessary, you know. In

fact, I was rather looking forward to my first experience at skinny-dipping."

Zoe looked away from his piercing stare. She cleared her throat which had suddenly gone dry.

"Help yourself. As I said, I'll go and get my suit."

Ian laughed. "In that case, I'll get mine. I don't think skinny-dipping alone would be much fun."

Later they shared a lunch of sandwiches in the gazebo. They had both decided an hour in the water and the sun was more than enough. They had barely finished eating when Zoe's physical discomfort started getting unbearable.

"I think I need to take a shower. The salt and sand are beginning to get to me."

Ian nodded. "I've been planning to install an outdoor shower to rinse off immediately. I just haven't gotten around to it."

He rose and picked up the tray that held the remains of their meal. Zoe followed him, carrying their towels. She left him to handle the kitchen duties and went to wash the sand and salt from her body.

She had just stepped from the shower when he knocked on her door. Wrapping herself in a towel, she opened the door to find him similiarly attired, her blanket from the previous night draped over his arm.

Ian eyed the bottle of lotion in her hand. He had performed the pleasant task of assisting her with the sunscreen earlier. Of course, that had only involved the areas not covered by her swimsuit. Lotion would need to be applied to every part of her body.

"I came to return the blanket, not that I expect you to need it again." The excuse sounded weak, even to his ears, but she did not appear to notice.

"Shall I help you with that?" he asked, indicating the bottle.

Zoe looked at the lotion. "Help me?"

He nodded. "There are areas that you can't possibly reach yourself. Just like with the sunscreen."

Zoe was mesmerized by the passion burning in his eyes. The blood rushed through her veins and she felt a sudden need to turn up the air conditioning that usually kept the house quite comfortable.

Ian hesitated, unable to tear his eyes away from her. He could almost feel the electricity in the air. He gently took the bottle from her and raised her hand to his lips, before lifting her in his arms and carrying her across the room.

He laid her gently on the bed and sat on the edge beside her. Slowly, he began massaging the lotion onto her body, first the arms. The towel was still in place, but barely covered the tops of her thighs, which were the second area to receive his attention. His hands roamed lightly over her body, but the gentle friction had the same effect as rubbing two sticks together. The difference was that the fire being created was in her body.

When he finished ministering to her limbs, Ian leaned over and kissed her. His tongue outlined her lips before he claimed them. When he started to withdraw, Zoe protested, wrapping her arms more tightly around his neck. Ian would not be denied his exploration, gently loosening her hold.

He sat up and, a moment later, the towel no longer shielded her from his view. Zoe watched him as his gaze traveled the length of her body, from her neck to her feet. His finger traced a line, beginning at her toes and traveling slowly up her leg, pausing at the triangle of curls before continuing its journey.

He finally picked up the lotion once again. Urging her onto her stomach, he resumed his tender massage. Not an inch of her body was neglected. Each stroke fueled the fire burning in every nerve of her body. By the time he turned her onto her back again, Zoe wondered if a person could die of sheer pleasure.

Ian had no intention of rushing her pleasure, or his own. The lightning of the previous night had only given him glimpses of her considerable physical beauty. The small slivers of dawn's light that found their way through the opening in the drapes had not been much more helpful. Now, with the sun streaming through the glass doors, nothing was hidden from his gaze. His hands moved over her body, caressing and exploring, seeking out all of her hidden treasures.

Zoe writhed beneath his touch. When his fingers entered her wet sheath, she moaned. He turned away from her then, but just long enough to open the foil package in the pocket of his towel wrap. A moment later, they were locked in the age-old dance of love.

Later, their hunger sated, Zoe lay sleeping, wrapped in Ian's embrace. It occurred to him that he could be content to spend the next six months right there on the island with her. Unfortunately, he would not be permitted that luxury. Maybe later, after he had taken care of Chad and she had recovered her memory, there would be a chance for them.

It was almost two hours later when Zoe awakened from her nap. At first, she was a little surprised to find herself alone in the bed. When she noticed the time, she understood. She could hardly expect him to wait around for her to wake up. He had obviously not been exhausted by their activity. Or, maybe, he had just returned to his own room to sleep.

She rose, dressed, and went to see if that was the case. She found him in the library, reading. He looked up and set his book aside as she entered.

"Did you enjoy your nap?"

"Yes, but I feel a little guilty about being so lazy," she said, yawning. "I don't usually sleep in the middle of the day. I blamed it on the salt air when I first arrived. Maybe that's it. Or maybe I'm just getting lazy from doing nothing."

"Or, for today at least, you can blame it on the exercise," he suggested, grinning.

"In that case, I'd think you'd have been napping, too."

Ian stood up and walked over to her. His finger traced a line from her ear, down her neck and across her collarbone.

"I considered trying to do just that, but, actually, the exercise energizes me. Besides, I knew I had to leave that bed. Otherwise, who knows how long we might have been there."

Leaning down, he planted a brief kiss on her lips. The look in his eyes told her that he was not exaggerating.

"I think it's time to satisfy a different appetite. Let's go and see what we can find for dinner."

# CHAPTER SEVENTEEN

"Sharmane, you know I would never do anything to put your trust fund in jeopardy," Cal insisted.

He took her hands in his, looking into her eyes with such sincerity that his wife was beginning to feel guilty for hesitating.

"I've researched this investment, thoroughly. With the return we'll get, we'll be set for life. I promise you."

Cal had not wanted to involve his wife in his latest transaction. He had expected he would have enough for the purchase with the money he had "borrowed" from his clients. He would have, if the merchandise had not been ready sooner than he anticipated.

He had no intention of telling her what he really planned to do with her money, but he had to persuade her to give him the balance needed for the purchase. If he could not come up with the money, Burnett might not be able to find another buyer, especially at this late date.

Cal's determination was mostly based on the fact that the property belonged to Ian. Dear cousin Ian.

All his life he had heard about the accomplishments of

his brilliant cousin. Ian was valedictorian of his high school class. Ian had graduated summa cum laude from college. Ian had his own software company.

Cal had received a great deal of pleasure in stealing Ian's fiancée right from under his nose. He liked Sharmane. She was a beautiful, desirable woman, but he was not in love with her. He sometimes wondered if she was in love with him, but he never really gave much thought to that question. It was not that important.

In the beginning, he'd had no intention of marrying her. He had only planned to seduce her away from Ian, have an affair, and move on. That is, until he found out about her trust fund.

Her father had died when she was sixteen, after receiving a hefty accident settlement six months earlier. His will had left half of his estate to her. Most of the other half had still remained when her mother died five years later. Both estates had become available to her on her twenty-fifth birthday the previous year.

Even before he had hit on his latest scheme, the money had been enough of an inducement to propose marriage. Thanks to a good investment counselor, by that time it had amounted to close to five hundred thousand dollars.

Of course, when they became engaged she told him about the trust fund. She also insisted he take over her investments. When she told him about the money, he acted suitably surprised.

He could have simply "borrowed" those funds now, as he had with his other clients. He had covered his tracks well with that. Even if he should be suspected, he was smart enough not to have put the funds in a bank account. The interest he might have gained was not worth the possibility of having to explain the origins of such a large sum of money.

He had decided there was no need to embezzle his wife's funds, not yet anyway. That would be his last resort, if she refused.

He had been paving the way for this request from the beginning. When they became engaged, she had wanted to use part of it to buy a home. He convinced her that his six-figure income was more than sufficient for a comfortable lifestyle.

His suggestion was not based on any altruistic motive. Although he had known nothing of Ian's software, he had been in the investment business long enough to expect that large a sum of money would be more useful in the future. Aside from finding a better use for the money, he was also aware that refusing to use her money put him in a better light. If he came to her with a request later, she would be more likely to agree.

Everything was finally coming together. He needed her money to meet the price. He had to have that software.

Sharmane was only half listening to her husband's plea. She wanted to believe him. More than that, she wanted to trust him. She loved him, but she was not sure she trusted him. He was so handsome and charming.

Ian was handsome and charming, too. That had not been enough, though. She had been unable to make him understand that she needed more than he had been willing, or able, to give. In spite of that, she had convinced herself she was in love with him, until Cal started pursuing her.

She had planned to break her engagement before that terrible night, but had never been able to find the right words. She had not planned to make love with Cal that night. She had been angry and hurt when Ian called, breaking their date.

When Cal called later that same evening, her anger and disappointment had come pouring out. He had taken advantage of her distress and come to her apartment to offer consolation. That visit had ended with them in bed, and Ian walking in on them.

She had called Ian the next day, trying to explain. She was hurt, but not surprised, when he hung up on her. What excuse could she offer for her actions?

There had been moments after their breakup when she had questioned her actions. She had finally admitted to herself that she was not in love with Ian, but she was not sure she was in love with Cal, either.

Later, when she had fallen in love with Cal, she still had doubts about his feelings for her. When he proposed a year after her breakup with Ian, she had actually been a little surprised. At that time, she experienced a moment of suspicion that his proposal had something to do with her money, except that she had never told him it existed.

She felt a little guilty when she told him about the trust fund and offered to use it to buy a house for them, but he had refused. He insisted they live on his salary. How could she refuse him now? She was still hesitant about one detail, though.

"Do you have to invest it all, Cal?"

Even he could not be that greedy. He expected to make enough money from his investment to replace her funds many times over, but he could see that she was more likely to refuse if he insisted on the entire amount.

"Not all of it, baby. I need at least four hundred thousand, though. It's a big deal. Like I said, when it's completed we'll be set for life."

"Alright, Cal. Actually, it's no more than I'd have spent if you had agreed to let me buy the house."

Cal silently breathed a sigh of relief. He had not been looking forward to trying to explain to Burnett that he had been unable to raise the money. He had made a deal and he had the impression that Burnett was not the kind of man who would take kindly to having someone renege on a deal.

\* \* \*

"You wanted to see me, Keisha?" Chad asked, entering his supervisor's office.

"Yes, Chad. The manager at Omega called. He's quite upset that you haven't completed the job. We had estimated it would take three weeks. What's the problem this time? It's been more than a month."

"First of all, *we* didn't estimate that time frame. *You* did."

"The estimate was based on a number of similar jobs. The other analysts had no trouble finishing those jobs within the same period."

"Well, maybe the other analysts didn't run into the same problems I had. You know no two jobs are exactly alike."

Keisha had run out of patience. She had been trying to cope with this arrogant idiot for much too long. What had Ian been thinking of when he hired him?

"I'm well aware that the specifics of each job can be quite different. However, this is not the first time you missed a deadline. When Ian returns I'll have to discuss it with him, again."

For the first time since entering her office Chad began to feel a little uncertain about the security of his job. Under other circumstances, he would not have cared. He could always find another job, but at the moment, he could not afford to lose this one. Not until he got his hands on the software. After that, he did not plan to need a job at all.

"What do you mean, again? You've complained to him before?"

"As a matter of fact, I have. And you might as well know that he's not any more pleased with your performance than I am."

"Well, I'm sure he understands that deadlines can't always be met. I'll discuss it with him myself when he returns."

He turned to go. "If there's nothing else, I have to get back to work on the Omega job that you're so concerned about."

It was all Keisha could do to keep from throwing her paperweight at him. She had met a number of men like him in her life. She had never expected to have to deal with one of them on a daily basis. She might have been able to overlook his arrogance if he were half as intelligent as he thought he was.

Instead of going back to work, Chad went in search of Derek. He had to talk to Ian, and Derek was the only one who could arrange it. Derek was just about to enter his office when Chad walked up to him.

"I need to talk to you, Derek."

Something in Chad's voice alerted Derek to the possibility that there could be trouble with their plans. He was ready to plant the software. This was no time to have a wrench thrown into the works.

"Sure, Chad, come on in."

Once they were seated, Chad began to have second thoughts about discussing the problem with Derek. He hesitated.

"What's the problem, Chad?"

"Keisha. I asked Ian to move me from her unit months ago. I know he thinks I'm imagining things, or blowing them all out of proportion, but it's getting worse. From what she's telling me, she has him at the point where he's ready to fire me."

"I'm sure that's not true, Chad. Ian's given me no indication of that."

"I need to talk to him myself."

"Well, you know he's out of town. I don't expect him back for a few weeks. Can't it wait until then? Or suppose I call him and have him talk to you."

Chad shook his head. "No, I need to see him. I heard someone mention that he's on some island. Can you get him to come back earlier?"

Derek knew that was out of the question. Ian would not

return Zoe to the mainland until after Chad and his friends were in police custody. When they had met with Jared, Ian had mentioned that he did not like leaving her alone on the island. He certainly would not be pleased about having to leave her just to placate Chad.

"I don't think he'll do that. Why don't you just talk to him?"

"That's not enough, Derek. Keisha's been on my back for months. I know it's a lot to ask, but I really need to see him face to face. If I can see him face to face and he tells me that Keisha misunderstood, that he's not planning to get rid of me, I'll know I can believe him."

Derek sighed. He had no choice. Chad had obviously worked himself up and would not be content until he met with Ian.

"Alright, Chad. I can't make any promises, but I'll give him a call."

For almost a week, Ian and Zoe had enjoyed an idyllic interlude. Neither of them allowed any disturbing thoughts or doubts to intrude on their pleasure. They walked on the beach and explored the woods behind the house.

Ian was a little embarrassed to admit that he had not explored it on his own, except at the time he was planning the layout of the house. Zoe shared with him the special place she had discovered soon after her arrival on the island.

The nights, and most of the afternoons, were spent in each other's arms. Ian was amazed at the effect she had on him. No matter how often they made love, he could not get enough.

He had told her more about his family's acquisition of the island. He hesitated, as in the beginning, to speak of his family at all, but she asked so many questions. It was as if she was hoping that his stories about his family would jog her memory of her own. She insisted that she enjoyed hearing his stories, especially the ones that involved his grandmother.

Their peaceful interlude was interrupted when Ian received a telephone call from Derek. He was expecting the call to come when the plans were in place to snare Chad. Instead, his brother informed him that a problem had arisen that could call a halt to everything.

"Chad insists on seeing you. He's been having a problem with Keisha. I told you there's a personality clash between the two of them. Evidently, the problem has escalated."

"I think a lot of the problem is that Chad is one of those men who have a problem with female supervisors."

"That's probably true, but evidently the situation has really gotten blown out of proportion. He's gotten it into his head that you're on the verge of firing him. I told him that's not true, but he insists on hearing it from you.

"I suggested that he wait and see you when you return, or talk to you on the phone. Since I couldn't tell him when you'd be back, that didn't satisfy him. He insists on seeing you face to face. He found out where you are and I'm afraid he's wired up enough to get directions and come out to the island on his own."

"Where are we in terms of getting everything in place to spring the trap? Can't you stall him that long?"

"Actually, Ian, I'm all set to plant the fake software. The problem is that I don't know if he suspects something and this is just an excuse to assure himself that you really are away from the city. I'm afraid that if we don't go along with him, we may blow it. He may decide it's too risky."

"In that case, I'll meet you in Savannah the day after tomorrow."

The evening after his conversation with Derek, Ian had second thoughts about leaving Zoe alone. He had not wanted to make another trip to the mainland until the trap was set. At least, once that was done, everything would be out in the open and he could explain his actions.

The final decision was taken out of his hands. The weather forecast called for thunderstorms the following afternoon. He recalled Zoe's reaction to the previous storm. It also reminded him that he had been so engrossed in the developments in their relationship since then, that he had not checked the bungalow for storm damage.

An examination of the smaller building revealed two broken windows. Fortunately, they were in the tiled laundry room and the water damage was minimal. It would have to be fixed as soon as possible. The storm might not materialize, but it was best not to take that chance. He would have to change the meeting.

He returned to the main house and called Derek. After explaining the problem, he suggested, "We might have to postpone my meeting with Chad."

"That might not be a good idea, Ian. Unfortunately, I already mentioned it to him. If I call it off now, it might really spook him."

"Well, the only alternative is to bring him here and that could be risky. I can't let him see Zoe. If she was in on the scheme, he'll assume she's told us about it and that'll definitely scare him off."

"Do you really think it'll be that difficult to keep them apart? There's no need for Chad to go to the house. If we keep Zoe away from the dock, they're not likely to meet."

Ian mulled that over for a minute. There would have to be some reason to keep her busy at the house. Finally, Ian came up with a possible solution.

"Call me just before you leave and I'll come down to the dock as soon as I see the boat approaching. I'll tell Zoe you had to bring some papers for me to sign. If you bring some groceries, too, it will give you an excuse to come to the house. If necessary, you can keep her busy while I talk to Chad."

"Do you think that'll work?"

Ian sighed. "I admit it sounds a little shaky, but I can't think of anything else to do. You seem certain that it would jeopardize everything to put off the meeting and, with a possible storm coming, I can't put off the repairs to the bungalow."

# CHAPTER EIGHTEEN

As the boat approached the island, Chad watched from the deck. There were two figures on the beach, he assumed one of them was Ian. The other was obviously a woman. So, that's why Derek couldn't give him a definite day for Ian's return to Atlanta. He also now understood Ian's reluctance to have his little "vacation" interrupted.

He was curious about the woman. Even from this distance, he could see that her body left nothing to be desired. There was a pair of binoculars on one of the deck chairs. Chad picked them up and focused on the figures, specifically the woman.

When her face came into focus, he drew in his breath. Zoe! Burnett's spy from the warehouse who had so conveniently, and abruptly disappeared. Either that or someone who looked enough like her to be her twin. True, he had not had a prolonged look at her face in the warehouse, but he had seen it long enough to identify her.

What could she be doing here? Was it a coincidence? How much had she heard in the warehouse? Enough to warn Ian? What would he do if she came to the boat with Ian?

Chad forced himself to calm down and consider his questions logically. She couldn't have told Ian. If he knew there was a plan afoot to steal his precious software, he would hardly be taking time off for a romantic rendezvous. The fact that they were acquainted had to be a coincidence.

He speculated on possible options should she accompany Ian to the boat. He remembered his reason for the visit and came to the conclusion that his employer was not likely to involve her in their business. He was now confident that Ian would come alone. After all, this was not a social call. Ian was almost certain to want to keep the interruption to his tryst as brief as possible. The fact that he had been so secretive about his little vacation was evidence of that.

He had not wanted to make any waves on the job, not now. If Ian had assigned him a different supervisor when he asked him, this would have been unnecessary. He was afraid Keisha would have her way and he would be fired before he could get his hands on the software. Derek's efforts to placate him had been useless. He might be the boss's brother, but he was not the one in control.


The morning of Derek and Chad's visit Ian had informed Zoe he expected Derek early that afternoon. They ate lunch in the gazebo and were strolling on the beach when Derek's boat approached the island. They had had their usual morning dip in the ocean and both were still in their swimsuits, although Zoe had added a sarong cover-up.

Ian had talked her into staying out on the beach. He knew if he kept her from her shower, she was not likely to want to go with him to the boat. By that time, she would be eager to shower and remove the sand clinging to her.

"I'll let you go take care of your business. I'll get the lunch things from the gazebo on my way in. I need to get this sand washed off anyway. I'm starting to feel like an emery board."

"I shouldn't be long."

"Oh, sure. Probably just long enough for me to finish cleaning up from lunch."

Ian smiled and took her in his arms. After a lingering kiss, he patted her on the rear and, reluctantly, released her and stepped back.

"I hope Derek isn't in one of his talkative moods."

Zoe watched for a few minutes while the boat docked and Ian walked away toward the dock. Then she went to the gazebo, picked up the tray and went into the house. She had just finished putting away the leftover food when Derek entered, laden with grocery bags.

The sight of Zoe in a bathing suit, contentedly working in the kitchen, added more evidence to the idea that had formed in his mind concerning his brother's feelings. He did not doubt Ian's original reason for keeping her there. He was still willing to admit that his brother's foremost concern was the possible theft of the software, but there was a much more personal reason involved now.

"Hello, Zoe," he greeted her, setting the bags on the table.

"Hi, Derek. I thought you were just coming to bring some papers for Ian to sign."

"That was the main reason, but since I was coming anyway, he asked me to pick up a few things."

He started emptying the bags. She came to help and they worked together for a few minutes, until Zoe decided she had to get rid of the sand.

"I think I'll leave you to finish. I really can't take any more of this sand clinging to my skin."

"No problem. I'll be leaving soon. I'm sure Ian will be finished with those papers by the time I get back to the dock."

* * *

When Zoe entered the kitchen after her shower, Derek was gone, but Ian had not returned. She looked out the French doors and noticed the boat was still at the dock. She also noticed there were three men on deck. The fact that Derek had not mentioned bringing another person with him aroused her curiosity.

She retrieved the binoculars she had seen lying on the table in the living room. Returning to the kitchen, she trained them on the three men. When the stranger came into focus, Zoe gasped. It was the man from the warehouse!

That recognition was all that was necessary to trigger her memory. The events of that day flooded back into her mind. She recalled the conversation in the warehouse and the suspicions that had led up to that disastrous undertaking.

Her mind replayed the questions she had been unable to answer when she'd awakened on the sofa. They had told her that they found her lying on the floor and assumed she had hit her head on the doorjamb or the stairs. She remembered that she had been on her way up the stairs to try to sneak out through the window. Every detail of that frightening episode was now clear. The fear and apprehension she had felt with her memory loss was nothing compared to what she now experienced.

As if that was not bad enough, Zoe felt as though her whole world had been turned upside down with what she had just discovered. She could hardly believe what she was seeing. She did not want to believe it. Ian was part of the plot! There could be no other explanation. He was a thief!

Tears gathered in her eyes as the full impact of this discovery hit her. She shook her head in dismay. How could she have been so foolish as to get involved with a man about whom she knew next to nothing? She had no one to blame but herself. She had known it was not wise to let her feelings control her decision, but she had ignored that little voice of reason.

If nothing else, her amnesia should have made her more cautious. If her memory had been intact, the fact that his yacht was moored conveniently near the warehouse would have given her a clue. It would not have been proof, but it would have made her consider the evidence more carefully before acting. At least she liked to think that she would have been that sensible.

All of the pieces of the puzzle were falling into place. Just as Mr. Burnett's store had been a perfect cover for selling stolen merchandise, Ian owning a software company was a perfect cover for stealing software. How many times had he already gotten away with it? Whatever he stole could simply be passed off as one developed by his company.

Her ruminations raised other questions concerning her own plight. Was he just playing games with her? Did he actually know why she had been aboard his yacht? And if he knew that, what would he do when she recovered her memory? How dangerous were these people? Were they just involved in grand larceny, or would they go even further?

She unwillingly recalled their lovemaking. He had been so tender and caring. She could not bring herself to believe that he would really harm her. She had almost convinced herself that she was in no real danger when she remembered that he was not in it alone. Ian, himself, might not be a threat to her safety, but what about the others? What happened to her might not be his decision alone.

She tried to ease her apprehension with the idea that since they believed she had no memory of that day, they would have nothing to fear from her. Once they had the software in their possession, who was she to say he had not designed it? It would be her word against his. The more she thought about it, the more convinced she became that she was being paranoid.

She could easily fake her continued loss of memory so

as not to arouse his suspicion in that direction. The real
problem was their personal relationship. She could not
continue as usual. Even if she was inclined to overlook her
discovery and continue that relationship, she was bound
to give herself away during a moment of intimacy.

She had fallen in love with him, there was nothing she
could do about that. Even more troubling was the fact that
the knowledge that he was a thief did not alter her feelings.
On the other hand, now that she knew the truth about
him, she had to keep from becoming any more deeply
involved. She had to distance herself from him. But how
could she do that without raising his suspicions? She had
to come up with some explanation.

She lowered the binoculars and paced the kitchen.
When she heard the boat's motor starting up, she looked
out at the dock. Suddenly she realized she was still holding
the binoculars. It would never do for Ian to see her with
them. She returned them to the table in the living room.


When Ian entered the house she was in the library reading. He greeted her, but then continued to his bedroom.
She was still in the library when he returned from show-
ering and dressing.

He sat down beside her, draping his arm along the back
of the sofa. His hand slowly caressed her bare shoulder,
sending shivers down her spine. Zoe was a little upset
with herself. In spite of her latest discovery, his touch still
affected her. But then, why shouldn't it? She had already
acknowledged that she was still in love with him.

He leaned over and nuzzled her neck, murmuring,
"Now where were we before my brother interrupted us?"

She had thought of a way to avoid further intimacy, at
least for the time being. Unfortunately, his warm breath
against her neck was having its usual effect and she was
having difficulty getting the words out. She leaned slightly

away from him, but before she could offer an excuse he raised another issue.

Ian was a little surprised when she pulled away from him. It occurred to him that she worried about the same possibility that had entered his mind earlier. He had intended to broach the subject that afternoon, but was interrupted by Derek's arrival.

"There's something we need to discuss, Zoe. What happened the night of the storm, or maybe I should say early the next morning, took me by surprise. I think we both need to be prepared for the possible consequences of making love without taking precautions."

Zoe could guess what he was leading up to. She knew he was right, it was a subject that needed to be discussed. She was chagrinned to realize that she had not given a thought to their carelessness until that moment.

"Exactly which consequences are you referring to, Ian?"

"First of all, I can assure you that you don't have to worry about any disease. Until that night, I've always been very careful—and I mean, *always*. My only excuse for my neglect is that I was taken totally by surprise.

"Aside from that concern, though, there is the real possibility that you could be pregnant."

"After one time? I know it's possible, but I'm sure it would be highly unlikely."

"Maybe. I just want you to know that, if that turns out to be the case, you won't have to worry. I'll be here for you, and our child."

"I'm sure you have nothing to worry about, Ian. As a matter of fact I have definite proof of that. That's the good news. The bad news is that the welcome evidence is accompanied by the usual pain. So, I'm sure you'll understand that picking up where we left off is not uppermost in my mind right now."

"So, that's what's wrong with you. I knew you weren't yourself," he said, relieved that she was not brooding about their carelessness. The words had barely left his lips when he remembered the bad news she had mentioned.

"Do you always have pain? Is there anything I can get for you?"

He seemed so concerned, Zoe was beginning to feel guilty about her deception. She had to remind herself why it was necessary.

"I'll be fine in a few days. I took some aspirin. I think I will go lie down, though," she said, rising from the sofa. "I'll call you when dinner's ready."

After she left, Ian sat thinking about her assurance that they need not worry about any consequences from their rashness. He was surprised to realize that part of him was a little disappointed. When he had started talking about the possibility of her being pregnant, he realized that the idea pleased him.

During the entire time he had spent reassuring Chad, part of his mind had been on her. It had taken more time than he expected to convince his employee that he had no reason to fear for his job. He had even agreed to relocate him so Keisha would no longer be his supervisor. If all went well, in a few days the possibility of losing his job would be the least of Chad's concerns.

# CHAPTER NINETEEN

The day after his visit to Blake's Island, Chad called
Burnett. He had tried to convince himself that Zoe's presence on the island, and her obvious connection to Ian,
did not pose a threat. The more he thought about it, the
more convinced he became that he had to tell Burnett.
The phone rang four times before Burnett answered it.

"Yeah, Burnett here."

"Burnett, it's Gordon."

"What is it, Gordon. Another delay?"

"No, I'll have the merchandise within a week. I called
to tell you I found the woman."

"The woman?" It took a moment for the information
to register.

"You mean Zoe?"

"That's right, your former employee who could have
ruined this whole deal."

"I told you there was no need to spend any time looking
for her."

"I didn't spend any time looking for her. I just happened
to see her."

"Okay, Gordon. Where is she?"

Burnett had put Zoe out of his mind, convinced that she could not be a danger to his plans. With Chad's next statement he was not so sure.

"On an island. With Ian Roberts."

"She knows Roberts?"

"Evidently, they looked pretty cozy."

"What were you doing there? Is that where you went to get the merchandise?"

"No, I had to see Roberts to make sure I'd have a job long enough to get the merchandise. The witch I've had to work with for months was making threats like she planned to have me fired. I had to talk to Ian to make sure my job wasn't in jeopardy."

"The point is, going there was a stupid move. She could identify you. Even if she doesn't know what's going on, she could tell him about seeing you. He'd be bound to get suspicious about our plans."

"Take it easy, Burnett. How could I know she'd be there? Besides, she didn't see me. I saw her on the beach and was curious. I used the binoculars and recognized her. Evidently, she hasn't told him anything about the conversation in the warehouse."

"Well, it seems I was right. If she was with Roberts, she must not have told him anything or not enough for him to put it together anyway."

As soon as he made that statement, Burnett had another thought. This one was best kept to himself.

"Where is this island?"

"It's just a small piece of land, about thirty miles south of Savannah. Roberts owns it. He calls it Blake's Island, but I'm not sure it's on the map. Anyway, what difference does it make? She didn't look like she was planning to leave anytime soon. I told you they were pretty cozy."

"You're probably right. She must have figured it would be a good place to hide out since she doesn't really know enough to go to the police."

Chad hung up after assuring the other man that there would be no further unexpected delay. He sat there for a moment with a growing feeling of uneasiness. He was almost sorry he had told Burnett that he had seen Zoe with Ian.

He was beginning to wish he had never gotten involved in this deal at all, but there was no way he could back out now. If he had known what Burnett planned, Chad would have backed out and taken the risk of angering Burnett.

Burnett realized that Zoe might not be able to identify Gordon, but she could identify him. The first order of business was to find out the exact location of the island. It might not be on the map, but there had to be a deed giving its exact location.

He had no intention of making a move until he was sure Gordon had the merchandise, so he had time to obtain that information. Once he set up the meeting for the exchange, he would arrange to take care of her—and Roberts.

Ian was impatient for Derek and Jared to complete their arrangements to entrap Chad. The tension from waiting had increased considerably since his employee's visit to the island. In the back of his mind was the worry that all of their work to trap Chad would be useless. What if he was having second thoughts? What if he decided not to take the bait?

Ian was anxious to have the matter settled, to have Chad and Burnett in police custody. Now that the millennium software was ready to go, he was eager to return to his business. He could do nothing with the software as long as Chad thought he had stolen it. Of course, there was always the option of calling a halt to the entire plan. He could simply fire Chad and go on as usual.

That choice did not sit well with him. Aside from the fact that he wanted the thieves caught, there was still the little matter of his guest. One very good reason for not calling a halt to his plans was that he could not return to his business and leave her alone on the island. Neither could he take her back to the mainland until he knew the extent of her involvement.

If she was not implicated when the others were arrested, it would not really prove her innocence. On the other hand, it would be enough to give her the benefit of the doubt. She would then have time to regain her memory and explain her reasons for being aboard the *Queen Bea.* He wanted, with all his heart, to believe in her innocence, but the nagging doubts persisted. That was the other reason for his increased tension—and fear.

Only one thing was certain, he was in love with her. Whoever she was, whatever her involvement, nothing would change that. For his own satisfaction, however, he had to know the truth. Until those questions were answered, their relationship could not progress any further. It occurred to him that until her memory returned, there was little chance of that anyway.

In addition to those major problems, he had sensed a difference in her in the few days since Chad's visit. Maybe it was only his imagination, but, aside from avoiding intimacy, she seemed to be trying to avoid him completely. As chauvinistic as it seemed, he had chalked it up to her period. As a teenager, he had learned to stay out of his sister's way during that time of month.

Zoe's attitude was not really the same as what he observed with his sister, though. She was not particularly short-tempered or emotional, just aloof. She had discontinued their morning walks on the beach. When he questioned her about it she explained that she did not feel well, that the pain tablets she took did not completely relieve the cramps. She spent most of her time in her room.

She came out of seclusion for meals, but even then the conversation was very limited. She appeared preoccupied, but with what, he had no idea. He was relieved when the call came three days after Chad's visit.

"We're all set, Ian. Chad's phone is tapped and Jared is still tailing him. His contact in the police department has been alerted that we expect him to make his move soon, maybe even as soon as tomorrow.

"I'm sure he's discovered the combination to the safe. He conveniently had some papers he insisted needed to be kept there. Of course, he stayed in the room, talking, while I opened it."

He paused and Ian asked, "What is it, Derek?"

"I can't figure out if he's really as dense as he seems, or if he just thinks that we trust him implicitly because of his mother and Mom being friends."

"Well, when you get right down to it, if he decides not to go for it, we won't lose anything. The problem with that is that I'd have to fire him and I couldn't explain why without any proof.

"There's also the matter of the buyer, I'm very curious about his identity. As Jared said, for all of Burnett's illegal activities, it's not likely that he has the funds for a deal of this magnitude. The likelihood that he's a go-between is more realistic."

"I expect Chad will set up the meeting as soon as he has the package in his hands. That means you'll have to be ready to move as soon as I call. We're guessing that the meeting will take place in Burnett's warehouse, but we won't know for sure until Chad makes the call."

"I'll be ready."

Zoe first became aware Ian had noticed the change in her attitude when he questioned her about their morning walks. That did not worry her, as long as he did not suspect the real reason for her withdrawal.

Trying to sort through her confused feelings was causing her enough worry. It was the hardest task that had ever been forced upon her. In spite of everything, she still loved him, still wanted him.

Could she learn to overlook the fact that he was a thief? Part of her wished she could ignore the little voice in her head that urged her to end her involvement with him. She wanted desperately to believe that it made no difference, that she could learn to live with it. She could pretend she knew nothing about his extracurricular activities.

When she considered that possibility, the little voice reminded her that she had not been able to overlook Mr. Burnett's questionable activities. That was what had gotten her into this mess in the first place.

But then, she was not in love with Mr. Burnett. Being in love with Ian should make it easier for her to overlook his faults. Instead, it had the opposite effect. She knew that his deception and dishonesty would always be in the back of her mind. She would never be able to trust him, not with what she now knew about him.

It occurred to her that his deception might have carried over into their relationship. He had never made any mention of love. Even if he had, she would not trust his words.

Her only hope was that eventually her love for him would fade. She had to get over him. She had no choice. In order to do that, she needed time and distance.

That was the other problem. How long could she keep him at a distance without arousing his suspicion? She had surprised herself by coming up with an excuse on such short notice. Unfortunately, it had its limitations. Within a week, at the most, she would have to think of another reason for keeping him at a distance.

Zoe was already having difficulty maintaining her deception. She had resorted to keeping to her room to avoid having to constantly fake the cramps and ill feeling.

\* \* \*

"Taylor, it's Burnett. You got the money?"

"It's available. I can get to it within twenty-four hours. Do you have the merchandise?"

"I'll have it tomorrow. We'll meet at the warehouse at seven."

"I'll be there."

Cal hung up the phone and smiled. His cousin's precious software would soon be his. Aside from getting the best of his cousin and making a mint in the process, he would have the prestige of being identified as its designer.

Two days after his conversation with Derek, Ian received another telephone call. This time it was Jared.

"The meeting is scheduled for this evening at seven, Ian. As I expected, Chad and Burnett are meeting the buyer at the warehouse. I've alerted Emmett and he's been in touch with Sgt. Travers. He'll bring a few officers with him to stake out the warehouse well ahead of time. If it looks like Burnett plans to call in some of his muscle, he can call for backup. He seems to feel that as far as Burnett is concerned this transaction is tame enough to handle alone. He's not likely to involve any of his less reputable cohorts.

"Derek and I will meet you at the dock. If you can arrive by four o'clock, we'll have time to grab something to eat before we meet with Travers to go over his plans.

"Travers wasn't too thrilled about having us around, but Emmett convinced him that we had earned the right to be there since it was your plan. He reminded him that you did them a big favor by discovering the warehouse where they now believe Burnett's storing stolen merchandise.

"You're the one responsible for that. If he hadn't chosen that as his meeting place with Chad, we wouldn't have known about it either."

"The plan sounds fine, Jared. I'll be there at four." He sighed heavily. "I'll be glad when this night is over."

After Ian hung up the phone, it occurred to him that Jared had not questioned him about his plans for Zoe. He had briefly considered taking her with him, but vetoed that option almost immediately. Even though Travers considered it only a remote possibility that there would be any danger, the potential was there. He did not want to risk the chance of her being hurt.

Although he still tried to ignore it, in the back of his mind was the possibility that she was involved. If that was the case, Burnett might see her and implicate her. For Ian, the bottom line was that he no longer cared what part she had played in the theft, he did not want her arrested. He was determined to protect her from that, if he could.

He knew that Zoe would not be happy when she learned he would be making another trip to the mainland without her. After the previous fiasco, he could not bring himself to believe that she would repeat her attempt get off the island on her own. Nevertheless, he pocketed the keys to the tender as a precaution. He also waited until the last possible moment to give her the news.


Lunch was an unusually quiet meal. Zoe admitted to herself that the lack of conversation between them in the last few days had been mostly her fault. This time, though, she noticed that Ian appeared preoccupied.

After lunch she retreated to the library to read, but was interrupted a short time later. She looked up from her book as he entered the room.

"I'm leaving for the mainland. I expect to be gone a few hours, but I'll be back tonight."

Zoe just stared at him for a moment before looking away. She said nothing. There was nothing to say. For the first time since she had come to the island she was content to be left behind. She guessed that he was meeting with his cohorts. If that was the case, she did not want to run the risk of being seen and identified by the stranger from the warehouse. She realized there was also a possibility Mr. Burnett would be there. In any event, she reasoned that she was probably safer on the island.

Jared and Derek were waiting for Ian at the dock when he left the *Queen Bea*. Ian had tried to concentrate on what was ahead for him that evening. In spite of his efforts, his thoughts remained with the woman he had left behind. He could not get her out of his mind.

Her reaction to being left behind had unnerved him. He was not quite sure what he had expected, but he had certainly expected some reaction, or at least a verbal response. He had been totally unprepared to have his announcement ignored so completely. If the keys to the tender were not in his pocket, he would be concerned that she might attempt leaving the island on her own again.

Ian felt the first stirrings of apprehension since he had first discovered that there was a plan afoot to steal the millennium software. Until now it had been all plans and little action on his part. He was beginning to comprehend the full weight of what he had started when he set out to trap the thieves.

Derek waved to him as he walked up the pier. When he reached the car he realized that Jared and Derek were accompanied by a third man.

"This is Emmett Powers, Ian. He'll explain the police procedure and what will be expected of us. We'll join Sgt. Travers and his men at the stakeout about an hour before the meeting."

They proceeded to the hotel as planned. Jared had decided that, as previously, it would afford more privacy for their discussion. Once settled in the room, Emmett opened a map of the area where the warehouse was located. The police would be covering all exits.

"It's best if we cover all bases," Emmett explained, "although from what Jared's told me, he always uses the same entrance."

"I've tailed him to the warehouse several times," Jared explained. "He always used the same entrance, the one on the street side, as opposed to the one facing the dock area." He shrugged. "Emmett and Sgt. Travers agree that there's no reason to expect him to change his habit this time, but we can never be sure."

"I think we all agree that Burnett is a middle man. Do you or Travers have any guesses as to the identity of the buyer?"

Both Emmett and Jared shook their heads. Emmett answered, "None. Travers has had a police tail on Burnett since Jared told me he was Chad's contact. Other than the warehouse, the only evidence he's come up with is the possibility that he's fencing some of the goods through a few pawn-shops. He's not listed as their owner, but they suspect the owners are only fronting for him. The electronics store seems to be his only legitimate business."

Emmett's last statement captured Ian's attention. Jared had said that Zoe was the manager for the store. If the store was legitimate, she might very well know nothing about Burnett's illegal activities.

"Are you sure about that, about the store being legitimate?"

"They can't really be sure of that until they do an inventory of the merchandise after the arrest, but that's their guess. They've held off taking any action until the software deal is finished. They figure it will give them that much more against him." Emmett continued, "Even with his hands in so many pies, Burnett is relatively small potatoes, moneywise. They have found out that he has some pretty rough contacts, though."

His statement reinforced the wisdom of Ian's decision to leave Zoe behind. Travers had noted that it was unlikely Burnett would have any of his muscle around for this transaction. Considering his basic character, however, he was glad he had not taken that chance.

# CHAPTER TWENTY

It was a few minutes before seven when the four men joined Sgt. Travers. He and a few officers had positioned themselves in an empty building across from the warehouse. Other officers were stationed in strategic points around the warehouse.

"We'll wait until they emerge from the warehouse after the deal is complete," Travers informed them. "We have to catch the buyer with the software and Burnett and Gordon with the money.

"Tell me something, Roberts. You could have settled for preventing the software from being stolen. Why all this?"

Ian shrugged. "I have to be honest, it's partly anger. I hired this guy as a favor, in spite the fact that his credentials weren't quite up to my standards.

"The other reason is more objective. I could fire him, but he'd probably move on and pull the same stunt somewhere else. When I first suspected him of stealing the plans for a computer game, I did some checking with his former employer. He beat around the bush, but I got the impression that Chad was asked to resign."

He had barely finished his statement when one of the officers called out, "We've got some activity over there, Sergeant. Burnett just arrived."

"Is he alone?" he asked, walking over to the window.

"Yes, sir. I guess you were right, he decided this transaction was tame enough that he wouldn't need his goons."

Ian joined them at the window in time to see Burnett get out of his car. He mounted the stairs leading to the door and looked around briefly before unlocking the door and disappearing into the building.

Ian tried to concentrate on the business at hand, but he could not keep his thoughts from wandering to Zoe. All along he had convinced himself that he would tell her the whole story after Chad and his cohorts were in custody. It occurred to him now that explaining why he had kept her on the island would reveal the fact that he suspected her of being a thief. How could he make her understand that it was a perfectly normal reaction, considering the circumstances?

His thoughts were interrupted by the arrival of Chad. He, too, looked around before entering the building. As Ian watched the young man, he felt his anger dissipating. It was replaced with a mixture of sorrow, disgust, and maybe just a small amount of pity for the young man. He had been given more than one opportunity to succeed, to make something of himself. Instead, he had chosen the quick, easy, and illegal path to success.

The majority of Ian's sympathy was reserved for Chad's family, especially his mother. He could imagine what her son's arrest would do to her, what it would do to any caring mother.

Ian had no idea what the effect would be on her friendship with his own mother. Would she accept the fact that it was Chad's own fault, or would she try to blame Ian? Whatever excuse Chad's mother might try to make for her son, Ian knew his mother would understand that he had no choice.

While Ian mulled over that particular situation, his eyes were on the warehouse across the street. They were waiting for the arrival of the buyer. Within a few minutes of Chad's arrival, a silver Mercedes pulled up and parked behind Burnett's Lincoln.

When the driver stepped out, Ian drew in his breath. Cal! He thought the situation was bad with the son of his mother's friend involved. That was nothing. Evidently, his cousin was the buyer. Where did Cal get the kind of money that would be needed for such a purchase?

That question led to a very unpleasant speculation. Ian did not like the direction his thoughts were taking. He recalled that Sharmane had inherited a great deal of money from her parents. Did that mean that she was involved in this?

There was also the fact that Cal was an investment broker. He imagined that anyone who would stoop to buying stolen software, would not balk at a little embezzlement of his client's funds, or worse. Who knew what means he had used to raise the money. Ian shook his head in disgust and disbelief as he watched his cousin enter the warehouse.

Chad looked around as he entered the warehouse, briefcase in hand. He had decided this would be his final deal with Burnett, maybe his final deal, period. Maybe it was the magnitude of this particular deal, but these deals were getting too nerve-racking. He had never been this nervous before.

Burnett was waiting inside, alone. Evidently, the buyer had not arrived.

"You got the merchandise?"

"It's right here. Where's the buyer?"

Burnett looked at his watch. "He'll be here."

Chad looked at the brand new computer sitting on the desk. It looked totally out of place in the dingy cubicle.

"What's that for?"

Burnett snorted. "Did you think he'd lay out this kind of money without testing the product?"

"I already tested it. It works perfectly. Of course, I realize that neither of you would take my word for it."

Just then, they heard footsteps. A few minutes later, Cal appeared and the transaction was underway.

After the software had been tested to Cal's satisfaction, he handed over the money in his briefcase and replaced it with the package Chad had brought. He had it! He had actually pulled it off.

He spared a moment to look Chad over. He was obviously not very bright. He could guess that Burnett was not paying him anything near what the software was worth. Even Burnett had lacked the vision to understand the full value of it.

They were preparing to leave when it occurred to Chad that Zoe might not be able to identify him, but she could identify her former employer. He had no intention of mentioning this to Burnett, but it was unnecessary.

"Thanks for the tip about our little witness, Gordon."

Chad was overcome with the same feeling of uneasiness that had been plaguing him for days. He was afraid to ask any more questions. He did not want to consider the possibilities. However, Burnett was so pleased with himself that he could not keep his brilliant plan to himself.

"She could've caused quite a problem, but I took care of that possibility. I took care of Roberts, too."

"What do you mean? What did you do?"

"There's a couple of men on their way to that island now. Neither one of us will have to worry about witnesses."

Chad felt sick. He had never intended for anyone to get hurt. It was supposed to be a simple theft. He grabbed the case that contained his payment. He had to get away from here, far away, and fast.

* * *

Less than an hour after entering the warehouse, all three men emerged from the building. Sgt. Travers and his men had them surrounded and in custody before they reached their cars.

"What is this?" Burnett blustered.

"You're under arrest for trafficking in stolen goods. Aside from the stolen software you just purchased, we have reason to believe the inventory inside will prove most interesting. Read him his rights, Officer Davis."

Ian walked over to his cousin. "Why, Cal?"

Cal sneered. "I have nothing to say until I talk to my attorney."

Ian walked away. Chad noticed his employer among the officers surrounding them. He turned on Burnett, forgetting his opposition to the plan the other man had revealed minutes earlier.

"You said you were taking care of him and the girl! You said she was no danger, even when I told you how cozy they were on that island. Then you decided not to take that chance. So what's he doing here? What happened to your beautiful plan?"

Ian heard him and felt his first flutters of fear. He closed in on Chad, who attempted to step back when he saw the look in Ian's eyes and realized that he had just implicated himself in more than a theft. He was prevented by the officer who had just finished handcuffing him.

"What do you know about the girl?"

Chad hesitated, looking around.

Ian's face was just inches away. "Spill it, Chad."

"I . . . I saw her and recognized her when I came to the island. She was in the warehouse one day when I was meeting with Burnett. She just seemed to disappear after that. We didn't know where she was until I saw her with you."

"What exactly did you mean about Burnett taking care of us? What was he planning to do, Chad?"

Before he could speak, Burnett cut in. "Shut up, Gordon. They can't prove anything. Just keep your trap shut."

When Chad hesitated again, Ian grabbed his shirt. "You're in enough trouble already. If anything happens to Zoe . . ."

Chad knew he was right. He had enough problems without being involved in murder.

"I don't know what he planned. He just said that while we were taking care of business here, his men were taking care of you and the girl."

Chills traveled down Ian's spine. From what Chad said, those men must be on their way to the island, if not already there. Zoe was out there alone and unsuspecting. She had no memory of that meeting in the warehouse. She would have no reason to believe she was in danger.

He turned from Chad to find Emmett standing a few feet away. "You heard?"

"I heard his statement to Burnett. Sgt. Travers is already on the radio to the Coast Guard and the Department of Natural Resources. A helicopter will be here in a few minutes. Where is this island?"

For a while after Ian left, Zoe tried to continue reading, but not surprisingly, was unable to concentrate. She finally gave up. All she could think of was Ian. Was he really out there making arrangements to buy stolen software? Or was this the final step in the plans? Maybe at this moment, it was actually being delivered. Would it all be over when he returned?

If so, would he finally take her back to the mainland? Why had he kept her here, anyway? Did he find out, somehow, that she had overheard the plans in the warehouse? Maybe he had known her identity all along. What other reason could he have for keeping her away from the mainland, away from the police? If the police had helped her discover her identity, she would have informed them of the plot. At the time, she did not know Ian was involved, but giving her information to the police could have ruined their plans.

The questions running through her mind prompted the feelings of betrayal that she had felt when she saw him with the man from the warehouse. If he had only been using her because she was available, why had he pretended to care? She still found it hard to believe it had all been an act.

She knew she was not thinking logically. What had she expected? Did she really think that he had fallen in love with her in a few short months? She had made the mistake of judging his feelings by her own. Worse than that, maybe she was only rationalizing her own behavior, telling herself that she was in love.

She had never felt anything like this before. She wanted to be with him every moment, awake or asleep, to touch him, listen to his voice, or just feel his presence. When he smiled at her, she felt good, as if the sun had just peeked through the clouds. When he was not around, there was a void she had never before experienced. Was that what it meant to be in love? If not, it certainly had to be a close imitation.

Whatever this feeling was, it was no longer beautiful and exciting. It had become a burden. Perhaps, when she was back in her own world, she could forget him, and, eventually, this entire episode would become a blur.

The longer she contemplated her dilemma, the more restless she became. She left the house and strolled the beach for a while, before wandering into the woods. She found her special little place and sat down on the log. Unlike her other visits, this time she found no peace.

After a while, she made her way back toward the house, but stopped at the gazebo. Before long, the previous few sleepless nights and the gentle sound of the waves against the shore combined to induce lethargy. She stretched out on the cushioned bench and soon fell asleep.

* * *

More than two hours passed before Zoe awakened. The sun was setting and her stomach told her it was past dinnertime. *That's typical, Zoe. No matter what the situation, you never lose your appetite,* she reflected.

On her way to the house she noticed the sky in the distance was becoming dark with clouds. Ian had said he would return in a few hours. As confused as she was about her feelings for him, she hoped he arrived before the storm. She did not relish spending a stormy evening alone on this island.

The irony of her present situation did not escape her. In spite of her suspicions concerning Ian's illegal activities, it was a toss-up as to whether she preferred to spend the evening in his company or alone with a thunderstorm raging outside. The choice was especially difficult because she could not help remembering the outcome of the previous storm.

Along with the other memories, she now remembered the reason for her fear of storms. When she was five years old, she had become lost while on an outing with her family. She remembered being out in the middle of a field when the rain started. They had found her huddled under a tree, miraculously untouched by the lightning around her. Even though she now knew the reason for her fear, that knowledge did nothing to eliminate it.

Her stomach rumbled as she entered the house, reminding her that it had been a while since her last meal. At that moment, filling the void in her stomach took precedence over her worries about the approaching storm or her perplexing emotions.

Dusk was falling as she cleaned up after her meal. The lights at the pier had come on automatically, but there was no indication of Ian's return. She stood at the glass doors for a while before deciding that such an action was only increasing her anxiety. She knew from her experience earlier that trying to read was useless. She decided that watching a movie might be a more helpful distraction if and when the expected storm broke.

Two hours later the movie had ended and she had just about given up on Ian. She now had a whole new set of worries. What if he had been arrested by the police? Would he tell them that she was stranded on the island? Or would he keep that bit of information to himself for fear that kidnapping would be added to the charges?

She almost panicked at the thought of being stranded with no one even aware that she was there. Then she remembered the bungalow. Eventually, its residents, Ian's aunt and uncle, would return. They would receive quite a surprise to find her there, but, at least, she would be discovered and returned to Savannah.

She left the library and started down the hall, but stopped when she thought she heard a boat approaching. Retracing her steps, she went to the living room window. She could see a boat pulling up to the pier, but she did not recognize the vessel. It was neither the *Queen Bea* nor the cabin cruiser Derek had brought to the island the previous week. It occurred to her that it might be the bungalow's residents, although she could not understand why they would choose to make the trip in the dark.

She watched closely as the boat docked. A frown creased her forehead when two strange men stepped onto the pier. If they were Ian's friends, surely he would have told them that he would be away from the island. Maybe they had taken it upon themselves to pay a surprise visit.

Zoe went to the front door and locked it. Friends or no friends, she had no intention of allowing two strange men into the house. When she looked out the window again, the boat was tied up and the men were coming up the pier.

The two men had reached the end of the pier and were

standing beneath the lampposts. What she saw then told
her that locking the door was useless. Zoe thought she
must be mistaken when she saw the guns in their hands.
Her heart pounded as fear gripped her.

Who were they? Why were they here? She pushed aside
those questions. The possible answers were too terrifying
and dwelling on them would not help.

*Think, Zoe, think. Obviously a locked door will mean nothing.*
*You can't just sit here and wait for them to break in.*

The two men were now halfway up the beach. If she
went out the front door they would see her. Where could
she go? The woods! The idea of trying to hide in the woods
was not a great option, but it was all she had.

She hurried down the hall to her room. She was startled
by the sound of breaking glass and ran to the French doors.
Opening them quickly and quietly, she slipped out into
the darkness.

Heedless of the rain that was now falling steadily, she
ran around to the side of the house. She glanced toward
the front door. There was no sign of the men. Evidently,
they had already entered the house. She ran toward the
woods.

# CHAPTER
# TWENTY-ONE

The helicopter ride to the island was the worst fifteen minutes of Ian's life. To add to his anxiety, he had learned that Sgt. Travers's men had also discovered drugs in the warehouse. It was one thing to know that Burnett was dealing in stolen goods. In Ian's mind, the fact that drugs were involved made him more dangerous. Ian could not shake the image of Zoe, alone and frightened, and in danger of her life. And it was his fault.

He had allowed Chad to come to the island, knowing there was a chance that he knew Zoe. He had assumed he could prevent him from seeing her. Of course, at the time, he had also assumed that she was on the side of the thieves. It would never have occurred to him that her only involvement was as a witness to what they had planned. It had also never occurred to him that their plan would involve anything more serious than theft.

After what seemed an eternity, the island finally came into view. Except for the porch light, the house appeared to be in total darkness. As the helicopter drew closer, Ian saw two men coming out of the house. They looked around, as if looking for something, or someone.

When one of the searchlights from the helicopter was aimed at the house, the two men gave up their quest and began running toward the pier. When Ian saw the men coming out of the house his fear for Zoe's safety increased, if that was possible. The aircraft had barely touched the ground before Ian jumped out and began running up the beach and across the lawn.

He reached the house, snatched open the door and ran through the rooms calling Zoe's name. There was no response and no sign of her. He was beginning to panic when he thought about the bungalow. He hurriedly found the flashlight and ran along the path. The bungalow was in total darkness, but he realized that she would not have been so foolish as to turn on the lights. He turned them on now as he went through the rooms, still calling her name again. There was still no sign of her and no response.

"Damn it, Zoe," he muttered to himself. "Where are you?"

As he walked back toward the house, he aimed the flashlight back and forth on the trees and shrubs around the structure. Surely, if she had been hiding in the shrubs she would have heard him calling and come out.

It was then that he remembered the woods to the side of the house. He made his way around the back of the house, shining the flashlight ahead of him. Just before he turned the corner of the house, the beam of light picked up footprints in the soft dirt. As he suspected, the footprints led to the woods. Ian picked up his pace and called to her again. She had to be in the woods. He prayed that he was right and that she was safe.


Zoe ran blindly through the trees, the blood pounding in her ears. She was so frightened she had not seen the searchlights or heard the motor of the helicopter. The image of men with guns searching for her stayed in her mind.

She was so intent upon escape that she did not hear her name being called or the footsteps in the brush behind her. She thought she had gone far enough into the woods to escape until Ian grabbed her arm, bringing her to an abrupt halt.

She screamed and turned to face her pursuer. Her mind was a jumble of questions when she recognized Ian. Tears of terror mingled with the rain streaming down her face. She struggled, trying to loosen his hold on her.

"Zoe, it's me. It's Ian."

"Let me go, please. I won't say anything to anyone. I promise. Just let me go."

A tumult of emotions hurtled through Ian. Relief that she was safe and guilt for being responsible for the danger she had faced. At first he was confused by her words, thinking she had not heard him, that she thought one of her pursuers had reached her. Grasping her arms, he assumed that her trembling was simply an aftermath of the ordeal she had experienced. She continued struggling and her next words sent a shock through him.

"Please, Ian. I don't care what you did. It's none of my business. I promise I won't say anything to anyone."

Ian realized that she *did* recognize him. She was shaking because the men on the beach were not the only reason for her fear. She was afraid of him!

"Zoe, I'm not going to hurt you," he assured her. "I came with the police. The Coast Guard is on the way and their helicopter is out there on the beach."

For the first time since sighting the two strangers, Zoe felt the terror slowly draining away. She was still hesitant. She had heard no helicopter. But then, she had not been aware of anything much, except her own fear.

"The . . . the police?"

"Yes, they're out there on the beach, taking those men into custody. Go and see for yourself."

He dropped his hands from her arms. Zoe still hesitated. Ian sighed. Obviously, she was not convinced that he was one of the "good guys."

"I saw those men leaving the house just as the helicopter was landing. I searched the house and the bungalow before it occurred to me that you might be hiding out here."

She still looked unsure. "Zoe, please. I promise you you're safe. You can't stay out here in the pouring rain. I'll go on ahead. If you follow me, you'll see the police on the beach."

He turned and walked slowly away from her. After a moment, she followed. She reached the edge of the woods and stopped, watching as Ian crossed the lawn. The house was brightly lit now, including the floodlights revealing the activity on the beach. She saw the waiting helicopter with the Coast Guard logo, just as he had told her. She started walking faster. A shiver went through her when she saw the two men, now handcuffed and guarded by one of the officers.

As she neared the group of men, Ian left them and started toward the house. Sgt. Travers met her halfway across the lawn.

"Miss Johnson? I'm Sgt. Travers. Are you alright?"

Zoe nodded. "Who are those men?"

"Friends of Frank Burnett," he explained. "How did you manage to get away from them?"

"I heard their boat. When I looked out and saw them, I ran into the woods. I hoped they'd get tired of looking for me and go away."

Travers nodded. He saw no reason to tell her that it was unlikely Burnett's men would have left without accomplishing their mission.

Before either of them could say any more, Ian returned with a rain poncho and gently draped it over Zoe's shoulders, although it was of little use since she was already soaked to the skin. She looked up at him.

"I'm sorry," she murmured.

He put his arm around her shoulders, squeezing gently. "It's alright, Zoe. Your reaction was understandable."

"I'll need official statements from both of you. I've been led to believe that you've known about Burnett for some time, Miss Johnson. You should have come to us. What you did was very dangerous."

Zoe looked away from his gaze. "I know that, now," she admitted softly.

"Well, the important thing is that you're safe, unless you catch pneumonia standing around out here in the rain. I think you've been through enough for one night. Your statements can wait until morning."

"I think you're right. Thanks, Travers. We'll be in to see you tomorrow. Any particular time?"

"Late morning will be fine. We'll be on our way now. I'll see you tomorrow."

As he walked away, Ian urged Zoe toward the house. By now they were both soaked through from the rain. Zoe had a dozen questions running through her mind. She was still a little shaky, even though the immediate danger was past. She was also beginning to feel the discomfort of being drenched to the skin. She shed her poncho in the foyer and handed it to Ian.

"I'm sure we both have a few questions, but they can wait a little longer. I think the first order of business is to get out of these wet clothes."


Half an hour later, Zoe returned from her room to find Ian pouring a mug of freshly brewed coffee. He poured a second one and held it out to her. She accepted it gratefully and went to sit at the table. Ian followed her.

She had almost reached the table when he asked, "When did your memory return?"

Zoe swung around, surprise written on her face. Until that moment she had forgotten that bit of information was news to him.

"Your statement to Sgt. Travers made it obvious that you remembered everything about Burnett. So, how long have you known?"

"Since the day Derek brought that man here. I recognized him from the warehouse. The whole episode came flooding back."

"That man is Chad Gordon. He works—worked—for me. What, exactly, happened in the warehouse?"

"I overheard him and Mr. Burnett planning to steal software, but that was all I could hear. I had no idea who owned the software, or how they planned to steal it.

"When I started to leave I knocked over some boxes and they heard me. They came after me. That's how I ended up on your yacht. I was running out of places to hide when I saw it. When the guard left the booth I sneaked aboard. I planned to leave as soon as they stopped looking for me."

"But Derek and I came aboard."

Zoe nodded. "You pulled away from the dock before I could sneak off the yacht."

Ian frowned. "I still don't understand how you managed to get caught up in this. What were you doing in the warehouse?"

Zoe hesitated, looking down into her mug. She recalled her family's admonitions about her impulsiveness.

"Zoe?"

"I worked for Mr. Burnett, managing his electronics store."

She continued to stare into her mug as she spoke. She hoped that explanation would be sufficient to satisfy him. Ian knew she was keeping something back.

"You mean he kept records of his stolen goods where anyone could find them? I don't understand why he would do that. I also can't understand why, if that's the case, the police haven't been able to get any evidence on him. Is that how you knew about the warehouse?''

"Not exactly. Evidently, fencing stolen merchandise was a real business for him. When I was looking for the legitimate inventory list I discovered an unfamiliar one that turned out to be the one for the stolen merchandise. It had an address for a warehouse that was also unfamiliar. That led me to suspect him of dealing in stolen merchandise.''

She knew she was getting in deeper and deeper with each question. She could almost hear the wheels turning in his head as he put two and two together.

Ian could hardly believe what he was beginning to suspect. Surely, she would not be that foolish.

"So, I'm back to my original question. What were you doing in the warehouse?''

Zoe sighed. She gave up trying to avoid telling him the real reason.

"I decided to check the warehouse myself, before calling the police.''

What he had guessed was true! Ian set down his coffee mug with a thump and glared at her. Zoe could feel his eyes on her, but refused to look up.

His voice was deceptively quiet when he responded to her admission, "You did what? I heard Sgt. Travers comment that you had known about Burnett, but I couldn't believe it meant what I suspected.''

"I couldn't go to the police without having some kind of evidence. I needed to see if the merchandise in the warehouse was included in the regular inventory.''

"Getting evidence is the job of the police. Do you have any idea how dangerous it was for you to go to that warehouse? And to go there alone was just plain reckless.''

"I know all that, now. Especially since Sgt. Travers said those two men were friends of Mr. Burnett.''

Zoe began to tremble, reliving the earlier terror. She

shook her head in disbelief. Putting down her mug, she rose from the table and began pacing.

"They were planning to kill me. All because of a computer game. It's unbelievable."

He went over to her and put his arms around her trembling body. Her distress was evidence that she needed no further lecture from him. Her ordeal had taught her a lesson.

"It's all over now, Zoe. You're safe."

He leaned back a few inches and looked down at her. "I would never have thought they'd go this far, either. It's amazing, though, what lengths people will go to in an effort to steal software games. In this case, I should have been more prepared, knowing that it was much more than just a game they were after."

He loosened his embrace and, placing his arm around her shoulders, urged her from the room. "Why don't we go into the living room? I'll explain."

Once settled on the sofa, Zoe relaxed. "You were going to explain about the software. You said it isn't a game. What is it?"

"As I said, the software they were after is much more important, and valuable, than any game. It's the answer to the problem many agencies and private companies are facing due to the coming millennium. With the six-digit dates in many computer records, the computer systems as they exist now, will be unable to distinguish twentieth century dates from twenty-first century dates. This software takes care of that problem."

Zoe's eyes widened as he described the way the software would perform this feat. "And your company owns the software?"

"That's right. I designed it."

He told her the whole story, including his suspicion of Chad. Then he explained the reason for his employee's visit to the island.

"Until this evening, I had no idea he had seen you."

"That's one thing I don't understand. How could he have known that *I* saw *him?*"

"He didn't. Now that you mention it, though, how did you see him?"

"When Derek went back to the boat I saw three people on board. He hadn't mentioned that someone was with him, only that he brought some papers for you to sign. I got the binoculars to see what was going on."

Ian shook his head. "Have you ever heard the saying, 'Curiosity killed the cat?' "

He regretted his choice of words as soon as he saw the stricken look on her face. He reached over and gently squeezed her hand.

"I'm sorry, Zoe."

She shrugged. "It's nothing I haven't heard a hundred times."

She wrinkled her forehead. "It doesn't make sense. If he had seen me with you on the island, why would they go ahead with their plans? Wouldn't he assume that I knew about the software and that I had told you about their plans?"

"I think when he told Burnett he had seen you, they did assume you had told me what you overheard. They couldn't know that when Chad saw you, you had no memory of them, or of the conversation in the warehouse.

"It never occurred to them that I already suspected Chad. Since no action was taken against Chad, they probably decided that I might suspect a plot, but I had no way of knowing he was involved. He knew you didn't know his name or anything about him. I guess with all of that, along with their greed, they decided to continue with their original plan."

"Except that Mr. Burnett decided to take the precaution of getting rid of me. Since he had seen me in the warehouse, he knew I could identify him as being involved."

"You really thought I had sent those men, didn't you?"

Zoe was not surprised that he raised that particular subject again. After her hysteria when he caught up with her in the woods, she could hardly deny it.

"What else could I think? I saw you talking to that man, Chad. I knew what he was planning," she insisted.

As she offered this explanation, another thought occurred to her. "Besides, what other reason would you have for keeping me here?"

It was now Ian's turn to be on the defensive. Her reasoning made sense. She had seen him talking to Chad and with what she knew of his employee, it was understandable that she would put two and two together and come up with five. He could only hope that she would see the logic in his reasons for detaining her.

"Ian?"

Before he could find the words to explain, she reached her own conclusion. "You suspected me of being in on the theft, didn't you?" she asked, pulling her hand from his grasp.

Ian sighed. Obviously, she did not see the logic in his suspicions.

"Please, try to understand, Zoe. It was a crucial time for me. I knew there was a plot afoot and, suddenly, this strange woman is found aboard the *Queen Bea*. What else would you expect me to think?"

"I don't know. Explain something, though. If you thought I was a thief, why didn't you take me with you so the police could arrest the whole 'gang?' "

"Because at that point, it didn't matter if you had been in on the original plan. You had been here long enough that you couldn't have been involved in the actual theft."

He wanted to tell her the truth, that he had no longer cared if she was involved. The last thing he wanted was to have her arrested, even if he knew she was guilty. He was in love with her, but it was too soon to voice those feelings.

"I suppose I should be grateful for that. Although, if you had taken me with you, I wouldn't have been in danger.

You haven't said it, but I think you were suspicious of me right up until the moment you learned I was in danger."

Zoe stood up and moved away from the sofa. She could not decide if she should be angry or hurt. What she actually felt was a mixture of the two.

"It doesn't matter, now. It's over, and I'm exhausted. I guess I was so keyed up, I'm just starting to feel it."

"Zoe . . ."

"Please, Ian. Just leave it alone. Good night."

"Good night, Zoe," he murmured as she walked away.

Ian sat there for a long time, considering his predicament. Her anger had been expected, he could cope with that. It was the hurt look in her eyes that really bothered him. When he had started to speak, he really had no idea what to say. She felt betrayed, and he could offer no further explanation to make her understand.

Aside from his feeling that it was still too soon for such an admission, he could not imagine confessing his love would help. First of all, it was unlikely that she would believe him, considering her present emotional state. It also occurred to him that her previous responses to him did not, necessarily, indicate anything more than a physical attraction. They needed more time, and a setting that was more normal than a secluded island.

You haven't eaten. But I think you were anxious to find out with all that happened, you looked." you at danger.

"You need to not have just been from the sofa. She could not during those she did not appreciate when she was left on the low extreme of the sofa.

It doesn't matter now. It's over, and I in relation to you was cooped up. But just wanting to bed did.

No—

Here, Jen, lie back and sleep. Good night."

"Good night, Zane" he murmured as she walked away.

Jen sat there for a long time considering his predicament. Her index had been expecting he could cope with that. It was the first look in her eyes that really troubled him. When he had started to speak, he really had no idea what to say. She felt unloved, and he could after promising an explanation no matter how difficult.

As he put his fingers through his tail he sent through his expression, he could not suppress. Somehow he had to reach help. Had he did it, it was unlikely that she could behave later, comforting her, she could also demanded to him that her grandmother, she felt she did not necessarily include anything more than explanation about them. They were no more close; and a sense that she was more normal than she could expand.

# CHAPTER
# TWENTY-TWO

Zoe awakened the next morning feeling confused. In spite of all that had happened, she no longer had any doubt about her feelings for Ian. She was still uncertain of the depth of his feelings for her, though.

She accepted his reasons for refusing to allow her to leave the island. What she did not understand was how he could make love to her if he suspected her of being a thief? Was she just a convenience, filling in his time here?

*You're not being fair, Zoe. You thought he was a thief, but that didn't make you stop loving him.*

She pushed aside her speculations, along with the covers, and got out of bed. By the time she had showered she had also reached a decision, of sorts. She realized that there was little she could do except wait and see what developed after they left the island. But what would she do if she never saw him again? *Silly question, Zoe. You'll pick yourself up and go on with your life. It won't be the end of the world.*

\* \* \*

Zoe entered the kitchen as Ian was putting a platter of bacon and sausage on the table. He was surprised to see her dressed in the same suit she had been wearing when she arrived on the island.

"I know we have to make our statements to the police, but I don't think you have to dress so formally. Are you sure you don't want to wear something more comfortable?"

"This is all I have."

Ian squelched the anger that arose. "You have the clothes I bought. Since I kept you here against your will, providing clothes for you was the least I could do. They weren't meant to be a loan. What did you think I would do with them?"

Zoe shrugged. "I hadn't really thought about that."

"I have a suitcase you can use. I'll get it later. You can wait until after breakfast to pack."

He walked back to the stove and returned with a platter of scrambled eggs. Zoe walked over to the counter and poured a mug of coffee. He stood beside her, waiting to freshen his own drink. She turned and looked up at him.

"I wasn't being petty, Ian. I really hadn't considered what was to be done with the clothes."

Ian shook his head. "You don't have to apologize. I can understand your confusion. I'm sorry I snapped at you," he said, taking her hand. "I guess we're both still a little on edge from last night's events."

Zoe looked down at his thumb, which was now caressing the knuckles of her hand. Sparks of desire flickered within her, reminding her of the passion that could easily burst into flames. That simple action reinforced her earlier conclusion. As incredible as it seemed, her love for him had been the only constant in this entire episode.

"Speaking of last night, Ian, I understand your dilemma in finding me aboard the *Queen Bea*. I guess we're even," she murmured. "We both jumped to conclusions."

Relief flooded through Ian. "You don't know how glad I am to hear you say that."

He took her in his arms and kissed her tenderly. He wanted to tell her how much he loved her, to hear her assure him that she felt the same. Lifting his head, he gazed into her eyes, seeking some some of that assurance. The passion was there, but he was unsure of any deeper emotions.

He cleared his throat. "Breakfast is getting cold and you still have to pack. Sgt. Travers will be expecting us before noon."

It took little time for Zoe to pack. She had stripped the bed and was preparing to put on fresh linens when Ian stopped her, assuring her that it was unnecessary. He took her bag and started toward the front door.

As she stepped into the hallway, she had one last glimpse of Ian's bedroom. She took a deep breath as memories of their nights of passion flooded her mind. She blinked back the tears. Those memories might be all she would ever have.

A short time later, they were aboard the yacht and Ian was manuevering the *Queen Bea* away from the dock. Zoe watched from on deck as the distance to the island increased. This time she was unable to keep a few tears from escaping. Grateful that Ian was engrossed in his duties, she quickly wiped them away. She took a deep breath and joined him on the bridge.

"You look surprisingly relaxed for someone who can't swim. Of course, considering that you came out here alone in a fourteen-foot dinghy, being out here on the *Queen Bea* should be a piece of cake."

Zoe glared at him. "You had to remind me of that, didn't you?"

"I couldn't resist it. It occurred to me this morning that you might be nervous about making this trip. Then I remembered your solo voyage. I also remembered how you became involved in this in the first place."

"I think I know where you're headed with this lecture, Ian. I don't want to hear it. I've heard enough of it all my life."

"I see," Ian said, nodding. "In that case, we'll change the subject. You have your memory back and you haven't told me anything about yourself. I understand you were working for Burnett?"

"Only temporarily, or at least it was supposed to be temporary. I was furloughed from my teaching job two years ago. That job came along and I decided to take it until something else opened up in teaching. I knew the unemployment insurance and my savings wouldn't last indefinitely, and I'd grown accustomed to things like eating and having a roof over my head."

The last part of her sentence was barely audible and Ian glanced at her. She looked stricken.

"What is it, Zoe? What's the matter?"

"It just occurred to me that I probably don't have that roof anymore. I haven't paid rent in months. I have an apartment in an old house and my landlords are a nice elderly couple, but I don't think anyone is that understanding. Especially since they haven't even heard from me."

"Stop worrying, Zoe. The rent's been paid."

"What do you mean? How do you know?"

Ian explained how he had discovered her address and sent Derek to take care of her rent. It never occurred to him that she would be unappreciative.

"You sent a strange man to pay my rent? I told you my landlords are an elderly couple. They're very old-fashioned. What do you think they'll assume from that?"

"Calm down. That same thought occurred to us. Derek told your landlord he was your brother and that you had been in an accident."

He could see that she was not totally satisfied with this information, but she accepted it as a better alternative to being evicted.

"You said you were a teacher. What did you teach?"

"Everything. I taught second grade. I really love teaching."

Something in her voice struck a chord in him. He remembered some of his own teachers, the ones who enjoyed their work. That enjoyment was obvious.

This new topic also reminded him that, although he had prevented her eviction, she was again jobless. At least that predicament was not through any fault of his, not directly anyway. Evidently, her lack of employment had not yet occurred to her. Before her mind wandered in that direction, he thought it might be best to change the subject again. It occurred to him that he still knew very little about her.

"Tell me about your family."

"My parents live in a suburb of Philadelphia. That's why it had seemed familiar when you mentioned Philadelphia. In fact, most of my family is still in Pennsylvania.

"And, in case you're interested, there is a specific reason for my unusual name. My parents' names are John and Mary. My mother was determined to give her children less ordinary names."

Ian glanced at her. "I hope you're not still upset about my comments. After all, you managed a pretty good comeback."

Zoe smiled. "No, I'm not upset."

When Zoe told him about her parents she remembered the trip they had been planning. She also remembered that they were planning to stop and see her on their return journey.

Sgt. Travers had mentioned nothing about her being reported missing. But then, if that wasn't his department, he might not be aware of that information. She would make it a point to check the records at the police station. If there was no report, she would assume her parents had not arrived in Savannah.

She put those thoughts aside and went on to tell him about her older brothers and sister.

"So, you're the baby of the family?"

Zoe glared at him. "That particular description has rubbed me the wrong way since I was ten years old. On top of that, my brothers and sister always felt they had the right to boss me around."

"Hmmm. That makes me wonder how many fights with your siblings were started by those words."

"I never fought. I could always find other ways to repay them," she replied, smiling at the memories.

Ian chuckled, nodding. "I can believe that."

"When it started raining last night, I remembered something else. I know why I don't like thunderstorms."

As she told him the story of getting lost, Ian smiled at her choice of words. She still refused to admit her fear.

They both fell silent after that. Each of them preoccupied with the memories of the night of passion that had followed that first thunderstorm.

Zoe started feeling nervous when they approached the marina. It was the same one that was near her boss's warehouse. The proximity to the place where her unwanted adventure had begun evoked even more tension. It also raised another question.

"I'm not really crazy about the idea, but could we go past the lot where I left my car? I'm realistic enough to expect that it's long gone, but at least we can check."

"I'm glad you realize it's a long shot. You are insured, aren't you?"

"Yes, I'm insured, but it would save a lot of aggravation if it had miraculously been overlooked by car thieves."

When they docked Ian informed her that he had left his car at his parents' home nearby. He called a taxi and they made their first stop the lot she had mentioned. As they expected, there was no sign of her car. Zoe shivered slightly when they passed the warehouse. Ian noticed and put his arm around her shoulders reassuringly.

Zoe had no idea what would be expected of her at the police station. She knew she would have to give a statement regarding the plot she had overheard. Beyond that, her responsibility was uncertain. Would she have to confront her boss? When it came time for the trial would she have to testify? She hoped that the police would have enough other evidence that her testimony would be unnecessary.

These questions led to more important concerns; namely, the problem of employment. Her job with Mr. Burnett had not been exactly what she wanted, but it had paid the bills. Of course, she could collect unemployment benefits again, for a while. Maybe this was actually a blessing in disguise. She would have to have faith that, this time, she would succeed in getting back into teaching.

After the trip to the lot to look for her car, the taxi ride to the house was short. It gave Zoe little time to prepare herself for the impending meeting. She breathed a sigh of relief when they arrived to find the house empty. Evidently, his parents and grandmother were away for the day.

It did not occur to her that Ian was as relieved as she to find the house empty. They knew he had been on Blake's Island for months and he did not relish explaining Zoe's presence. His mother and grandmother were bound to be consumed with questions.

Ian loaded the luggage into the car parked in the driveway and within an hour of leaving the yacht, they arrived at the police station. Once inside, they were directed to Sgt. Travers.

"Well, Miss Johnson, I'm glad to see that you seem to have recovered from your ordeal. I'll have someone take your statement so you can be on your way. I'm sure you're eager to return home."

He left the office for a few minutes and returned with two uniformed officers. "If you'll go with Officer Miller, Miss Johnson, he'll take your statement. Officer Dennis will take care of you, Ian."

Sgt. Travers's next statement was directed to Zoe as they rose to leave the room. "I'm afraid I have some bad news about your car, Miss Johnson. I checked our records. Your car had been reported abandoned in another part of town. Because the registration was current it wasn't destroyed. It's been towed to the impound, waiting for someone to claim it. According to the report, it appears that it's beyond salvaging."

Zoe shrugged. "That doesn't surprise me. At least it's insured. Thank you, Sgt. Travers."

Zoe followed the officer to a cubicle. She told him what had led her to suspect her employer of illegal activities and the events that transpired as a result of that discovery. She then answered his questions and was asked to wait while he checked to make sure they needed nothing more from her. A few minutes later he returned.

"You're all done, Miss Johnson. Sgt. Travers instructed me to take you home. He suggested we can stop at the impound if you like. The car itself is in pretty bad shape, but there may be some personal items still in it. If so, you can retrieve them."

Zoe was speechless, at first. She had expected that Ian would, at least, take her home. Obviously, he had better things to do. It appeared he was eager to wash his hands of her, the sooner, the better.

*Well, Zoe, that anwers your question. Evidently, you were right. You were only a convenient diversion.*

After giving his statement, Ian returned to the squad room in search of Zoe. There was no sign of her and he assumed she had not finished giving her statement. A few minutes later he was informed that she had left with the officer who had taken her statement.

Ian was stunned. She had seemed friendly enough on the trip to the mainland. He had assumed that they had laid to rest their previous animosity. He had counted on being able to continue their relationship, to get to know each other better. It appeared that he was the only one who wanted that.

Even if that were the case, she could have at least said good-bye. She had been in such a hurry to get away from him, she had left the clothes in his car. Maybe she had only given in to his advances because she felt she had no choice. It all came down to the fact that she had been held against her will. No matter that he was now in love with her, had loved her almost since the first time he laid eyes on her. He had lost her, and he had no one to blame but himself.

It was more than an hour after leaving the station when Officer Miller pulled up in front of an old brick house, the top floor of which was Zoe's apartment. She was thankful, and a little surprised, to have found her spare keys still in the little container under the fender of her car.

She had not relished the thought of facing her landlord with a request for him to let her into her apartment. Accident or no accident, it might be a bit difficult explaining why she did not have her key. She had hoped to avoid him altogether, but she was not to be that fortunate. He was sitting on the porch when they arrived.

"Miss Johnson, it's good to see you. We were gettin' real worried about you. Your brother said you were in a car accident. You been in the hospital all this time?"

"Oh, no, Mr. Everett. I've just been staying at my brother's house. He insisted I needed to recuperate."

"You doin' okay now?"

She noticed that he looked pointedly at the police car at the curb. She had prepared herself for his curiosity.

"I'm much better, thanks. The accident wasn't that bad. You know how older brothers are. They tend to be a little overprotective."

She nodded in the direction of the police car. "I had to give the police some information about the accident.

Since my car was in no shape to be driven, the officer brought me home.''

She waved at the police officer, who then pulled away from the curb. She pleaded exhaustion and managed to escape any further questions from her landlord.

# CHAPTER
# TWENTY-THREE

Zoe was apprehensive when she saw the light on her answer machine blinking as she entered her apartment. She played it back to find several messages from her sister. The messages gave her no real information, just an assurance that everyone in the family was well and a request to return the call.

Zoe knew she would have to contact her sister soon, but she put it off. She had to think of an excuse for waiting so long. Since Cleo had said nothing to the contrary, her parents must still be on the road.

Two days after her return to Savannah, Zoe had decided she could not put off calling her sister any longer. She had formulated an excuse in her mind, but was not quite satisfied that it sounded plausible. Before she could gather the nerve to actually place the call, Cleo called her.

"Hi, Zoe, it's Cleo. Is everything alright? I've been trying to reach you for weeks."

"Everything's fine," Zoe lied, keeping her fingers crossed. "Sorry about that. My answering machine hasn't been working right. It's been cutting off before the message is actually recorded. How is everyone there?''

The two sisters chatted for a few minutes. Zoe avoided any probing questions by mentioning her niece and nephew. As she expected, her sister went on for fifteen minutes about her children's latest exploits. She finally got around to the real reason for her call.

"I've been calling to let you know Mom and Dad won't be stopping in Savannah. Carl had a heart attack in New Mexico and will have to be flown back. Dolores will be flying back with him."

"That's a shame. How is he?"

"He'll be okay. It wasn't a severe attack. Anyway, Mom knew you'd be expecting them and she wanted me to give you a call. They weren't sure what they would do because he's been in the hospital. They only finalized their plans yesterday.

"Dolores was so upset about leaving Carl that Mom and Dad offered to drive the RV back home. Dolores suggested they take the RV and continue with the original itinerary, but they weren't comfortable with that, so they'll be driving straight home."

"When will they be home?"

"Probably not for a week or so. I'm sure Mom will give you a call herself."

Zoe heard her nephew in the background trying to get his mother's attention. "I'd better let you go and take care of your son's emergency. Thanks for calling, Cleo."

"There's always an emergency when I'm on the phone. You take care of yourself. I'll talk to you soon."

Zoe breathed a sigh of relief when she hung up the phone. She had avoided what would have been a major disaster. Her parents could have arrived and found her missing. Mr. Everett would then have informed them that she had been in an accident. That would not only have upset her parents, but would have raised the question with her landlord as to why her parents knew nothing about her mishap, especially since her "brother" had paid her rent. The whole thing would have snowballed and Zoe would have been hard pressed to come up with an explanation.

Even with that major problem resolved, she had been faced with the minor issue of anticipating her parents' reaction if they arrived and learned she was unemployed again. Now that there was no possibility of having to face them, she could avoid that subject.

Zoe had another reason to be thankful for her parents' change in plans when she received a package the day after her conversation with her sister. She did not notice the return address on the large box until she opened it to find the clothes she had worn on the island.

When Ian had practically deserted her at the police station, she had given no further thought to the clothes he insisted she keep. Fortunately, she had decided to wear her suit on her trip back to Savannah, in spite of his suggestion. The clothes were all there in the box, neatly folded and packed. He had even sent the straw hat, carefully stuffed with tissue paper. What was missing was any note of explanation. Why had he even bothered?

She stood there for a moment, staring at the contents. The memories and emotions flooded her mind and heart and a few tears trickled down her face. She wiped them away determinedly, closed the box and carried it to the closet. After shoving it to the back, out of sight, she sat down and had a good cry. Setting the box aside was the easy part. Shoving aside the memories would be much more difficult, if not impossible.

While Zoe was dealing with her problems, Ian was trying to get back into a work mode. He was kept busy with requests for his revolutionary software. Even he was slightly stunned at the volume of orders. Most government agencies and businesses had already begun the process of converting the dates in their files. However, they were woefully aware that it was impossible to complete the task before the turn of the century. His software would perform the task with time to spare.

Much of his staff was involved in this latest project, but he had a responsibility to his other clients and contracts. In addition to that, thoughts of Zoe were always in the back of his mind.

The day after he returned, he had started packing her clothes. Each article seemed to be premeated with the scent of gardenias or lavendar, reminding him of the nights and days she had spent in his arms.

He still could not believe that she had just turned her back on what they had together. But then, maybe what he thought they had was all in his mind. Maybe for her it was only physical desire after all.

As he performed his unpleasant task, he was so preoccupied with his thoughts that his answering machine clicked on before he was aware the telephone was ringing. He would have left it for the machine to take a message if he had not recognized his mother's voice. He had been expecting, and dreading her call. He knew she would want to discuss her friend's son and her nephew.

"Hi, Mom. I'm here."

"What are you doing, screening your calls?"

"No, I didn't hear the phone until the machine picked it up. How are you? How's Grandma?"

"We're all fine. How are you?"

"I've been better."

"With everything that's going on, that's about what I expected. I talked to Jane yesterday. You can imagine how upset she is."

Ian could think of nothing to say. Of course, he had known Chad's mother would be upset.

"I had no choice, Mom."

"Oh, Ian, honey. Do you think I called you to lay some kind of guilt trip on you? I know you had no choice. You did her, and me, a favor when you gave him a job. A good job. It's not your fault he turned out to be a thief."

"Thanks, Mom."

"As for your cousin, I can't say I was totally surprised by his part in this. I just feel sorry for Cole and Yvonne."

Ian felt sympathy for Cal's parents, too. In spite of all that had happened, he could even feel some sympathy for Sharmane.

"What about Sharmane?"

"Well, since you brought it up, she's taking it hard. It seems he had talked her out of a good bit of her trust fund for this deal. Did you know they just charged him with embezzlement, too?"

"Actually, Mom, I didn't know Cal was involved until the deal was underway. I can't say I'm surprised at any of it, though."

"It's a real mess, son."

"I know."

"Well, I thought you just needed to know that we understand why you did what you did."

"Thanks. That's all that really matters, Mom. I'm glad you called."

After he hung up the phone, Ian completed his task. He had known, deep down, that his mother would not have expected him to react any differently than he had. She had always drummed into her children's heads that each person had to take responsibility for his own actions.

That thought reminded him that he could very easily be facing some unpleasant consequences himself. Evidently, Zoe had been in such a hurry to get away she had forgotten her threat. Either that, or she had simply chosen not to have him charged with kidnapping. He supposed he should be thankful for that much. At the moment, that seemed of little importance.

Although he had expected the call from his mother, Ian would never have expected the call he received the next day. He had just completed a call from one of his buyers when the intercom buzzed.

"What is it, Karla?"

"Sharmane Taylor has been holding on line two. She insists on speaking to you."

Ian sighed. "I'll take it."

He hung up and pushed another button on the telephone.

"Hello, Sharmane." He stopped himself just in time from uttering the usual "How are you?" He already knew she was not taking Cal's arrest well.

"Hello, Ian." She hesitated, as if trying to find the right words. When she finally spoke, Ian detected from her voice that she was crying.

"I don't know why he did it, Ian. It's not as if we needed the money."

Ian could think of nothing to say. He could not make her understand that for some people no amount was ever enough. It was an affliction called greed. He could not believe she had called simply to cry on his shoulder. He waited patiently for the real reason.

"They won't even let him out on bail. They say there's too much of a risk that he'll run away. From what I've heard, you have some connections, Ian. Can't you talk to them?

"I know it's not a matter of you dropping the charges. The lawyer already explained that it's not up to you. You could talk to them about letting him out on bail, though."

"Sharmane, I don't have any control over that, either. The judge already made that determination."

"I see." There was another short pause. "Well, I guess there's nothing more to say."

"I'm sorry things turned out this way, Sharmane."

She hung up without another word. Ian put down the receiver and sat staring at it for a moment. He really was sorry for her. She would eventually have her money returned to her, but if she really was in love with Cal, that would be a small consolation.

Two weeks after her return to Savannah, Zoe was still trying to get her life back in order. She had been to several car dealers, but had not found a decent car to replace the one that had been destroyed. Without a job, she did not want to be burdened with car payments. She had finally received the payment from the insurance company, but since her car was more than a few years old, the payment she received from the insurance company limited her options severely.

She had experienced a bit of a hassle from the insurance company as to why she had waited so long to report it. She explained that she had been away and had not realized it was missing. She had the impression that they did not believe her story, but since her premiums were paid and they had the police report, they had no choice but to honor her claim. They had also been obligated to pay for a rental car for the time being, but she would have to find another car soon.

She had filed a claim for unemployment benefits and was working, diligently, to find another job teaching. She did not want to accept the possibility that she might have no better luck now than she had previously.

Her first step had been to contact a few of the school districts that already had her application on file. After that, she scanned the newspapers and sent out a dozen résumés for anything that was remotely connected with teaching.

Her first indication that her luck might be changing came with a response to a résumé she had sent to the director of a community center. She had almost missed the small ad in the newapaper, but the word "teacher" had caught her eye.

When she received a call to schedule an interview, she could hardly contain her excitement. The center was located in an area that had seen better days. For Zoe, the fact that she would be teaching made up for many of the less pleasant aspects of the job.

She met with the director, Mercy Lincoln, an attractive black woman who Zoe guessed to be in her early thirties. She explained that the center had been a dream of hers for years.

"I grew up not far from here. I was one of the lucky ones. I had good parents who worked hard and drummed into their children the importance of a good education. With their help, a few dedicated teachers and scholarships, I was able to finish college.

"This center is my attempt to give other children a chance to get out. Our location also makes it more convenient for hard-working parents. As far as I'm concerned, this is what it's all about."

Mercy explained that, in addition to a regular day care, the center offered a tutoring program after school. She was also in the process of arranging evening tutoring and a literacy program.

"Your résumé indicated that you taught elementary school. If you're hired, we could use you in the day care, as well as the after-school tutoring."

After she left the center, Zoe went over and over the interview all the way home. The pay was not great, but it would keep her solvent. More importantly, she would be teaching again.

The excitement she felt lasted well past the interview, although she tried not to get her hopes up. She had had no positive responses from any of the other résumés she had sent for teaching positions.

A week after her interview she returned from shopping to find a message from Mercy on her machine. She crossed her fingers as she dialed the number for the center. Mercy, herself, answered.

"I called to offer you the position," Mercy said, after Zoe

identified herself. "I hope you haven't accepted another offer."

"No, I haven't," Zoe assured her. "And I'm looking forward to working at the center."

"Good. Can you start as soon as next week?"

The two women discussed a few more of the details before ending the call. When she hung up, Zoe realized that her efforts to find a car might be more fruitful, now that she had a job.

In spite of her efforts, Zoe still had not made a decision on a car when she started work the following week. She had seen several possibilities, but had put off committing herself. She knew she was only delaying the inevitable, but she was not looking forward to having monthly car payments. She decided she might as well take advantage of the weeks she had left before her insurance coverage for the rental was exhausted.

The position at the center was as interesting as Zoe had expected, and even more tiring. She had forgotten what it was like coping with thirty children all day. She enjoyed the work with the preschool children, but her real joy came from the tutoring.

Her joy was tainted less than a week into her new job when she overheard a conversation between Mercy and one of the other employees.

"The computers Ian donated should arrive in a few days," Mercy explained. "I tried to talk him into coming down here to give the older students some basic instructions in their use, but I don't think he'll be able to get away from his company for a while. He did say he would send one of his employees, though."

"That's great, Mercy. You've really worked hard to make this center a success."

"I've had help from a lot of people. Aside from monetary donations, my friends have been very generous with their time."

It seemed to Zoe that there was no escaping Ian. She had

tried to put him out of her mind, without much success. On top of having this additional reminder, she now had reason to believe that he might be responsible for her being hired.

Obviously, he was Mercy's friend. It was hard to believe that it was merely a coincidence that one of his friends had been the only person to respond to her résumé.

She could not help wondering just how good a friend he was. Maybe they were even more than just friends. If so, what had he told her about Zoe? Probably nothing more than that she was an acquaintance in desperate need of employment. She obviously meant no more to him than that.

Zoe had a difficult time concentrating on her work the rest of the day. She imagined Ian asking his friend for a favor because he felt sorry for her. The last thing she wanted was his pity. She was tempted to quit the job, but that would certainly serve no useful purpose. Besides, she really enjoyed it.

# CHAPTER
# TWENTY-FOUR

The weekend after her first week at the center, Zoe faced a problem that outweighed any other consideration. She had good reason to believe that she was pregnant. She had had a few signs of that possibility earlier, but had pushed them to the back of her mind. Other problems had taken precedence. Now that she had the most important of those other problems solved, namely a job, she could no longer ignore this new discovery.

She remembered Ian's assurance that he would be there for her. She also remembered the excuse she had given him to avoid any further intimacy after she saw him with Chad. Even if she were so inclined, there was no way she could go to him now and tell him it had been a lie and she was pregnant with his child.

She considered the possibility that she might be mistaken. Maybe the stress and excitement were responsible for her dilemma. She told herself that, but it did not explain the sporadic queasiness she experienced. The first order of business was to see a doctor. She might be worrying for no reason.

Two days later she had her answer. She was pregnant. That was the unpleasant news. The good news was that she was healthy and everything appeared normal.

Fortunately, she had her job to keep her busy. At least it occupied her mind during the day. The nights were a different matter. She had never really managed to put Ian totally out of her mind, but with her latest discovery it seemed she thought of him constantly.

Before she had even seen the doctor, the idea of being a single mother caused some anxiety. Her first thought was the financial consideration. In the back of her mind she knew she could file for child support. She also knew she would have to be desperate before she asked Ian for a penny.

Her greatest concern was the emotional responsibility of raising a child alone. She would not allow herself to lose any sleep over it, though. There were thousands of women in that same boat and they managed to survive and raise good, decent children. She could handle it, too.

Within a few days after her appointment with the doctor, her feelings began to change. She no longer worried about whether or not she could cope with the changes and responsibility involved in raising a child.

The confirmation of her pregnancy had not been welcome, but she was getting used to the idea. She was even starting to enjoy the idea of having Ian's child. She still had no intention of asking him for help. She would have to tell him about the child, eventually. She could not be so unfair as to keep them from each other.

She was beginning to think that her new job and preparing for the child would keep her so busy she would have little time to indulge in self-pity. She had almost convinced herself of that when she received another unexpected delivery. She had just returned from grocery shopping when there was a knock at her door. She opened it to find a strange man on her doorstep.

"Miss Johnson? Miss Zoe Jonhson?"

"Yes, I'm Zoe Johnson."

"I have a delivery for you."

"A delivery?" she asked, looking at his hands, empty except for a few papers on a clipboard.

"Where is it?"

"It's parked downstairs, at the curb. I need you to sign here, please."

"Wait a minute. What do you mean, 'it's parked at the curb?' "

"It's a car. If you'll sign these papers, I'll give you the keys and the papers and be on my way."

"Look, Mr. . . . ."

"Mr. Samuels. The car was purchased as a gift and we were instructed to deliver it to you."

Zoe looked at the papers for the first time. The name of the buyer did not surprise her, Ian Roberts. This was the final straw! First he used her, then he dumped her, and now he decided to throw her a few crumbs.

Why? He couldn't still feel guilty about detaining her on the island. She had assured him that she understood his reasons for that. In fact, they both agreed that if he had not kept her on the island, Mr. Burnett's thugs would have succeeded in getting rid of her. Why couldn't he just leave her alone and stop meddling in her life?

Mr. Samuels's voice broke into her thoughts. "Miss Johnson? I need your signature."

"Take it back."

"I beg your pardon?"

"I said, take it back. I didn't order a car, and I don't want it."

"I can't do that. It's already been paid for. It's registered to you and the title is in your name. It's even been fully insured. If you don't want it, can't you just tell Mr. Roberts?" he pleaded.

He did not relish the idea of going back to his boss and informing him that the sale had to be canceled.

Zoe was beginning to feel sorry for Mr. Samuels. After

all, he was caught up in the middle. What was that old saying about shooting the messenger? That's all he was, the messenger. He was only doing his job. She signed the papers and accepted the keys.

After he left, she looked at the papers more closely. Sure enough, the title was there and a receipt indicating an insurance policy paid in full for one year. When she read the information, she became even more infuriated. He couldn't go out and buy a modest used car. The title was for an expensive luxury sedan, obviously much more than a crumb.

She had no doubt he could afford it. She had already seen examples of his financial success. In addition to that, from what he had told her, his latest software design, alone, would probably enable him to make a purchase of this kind as easily as she might purchase a television set.

That fact had, subconsciously, influenced her decision not to tell him about the baby. She did not want to him, or his family, to think she was after his money.


During the next few days Zoe's resentment increased. It was impossible to ignore the vehicle sitting at the curb. Each time she exited or entered her apartment she looked at it and was reminded of Ian's high-handedness. She had refused to drive it.

Her landlord was usually sitting on the porch when she returned home from work. She had noticed him eying the car since the day it was delivered. It took him a few days to finally ask her about it. She told him that she had won it in a contest. She explained that she was not using it because it was not yet insured and she was undecided whether to keep it or sell it.

At one point she had actually entertained the thought of selling it. The money would certainly come in handy in the future. She could even tell herself that the money would be used to support his child. On the other hand, she could not imagine he would refuse to support his child when it was born and, if necessary, proven to be his.

By the end of the week, she knew what she had to do. When she arrived at work on Thursday, she went directly to talk to Mercy.

"Good morning, Zoe."

"Good morning, Mercy. I came in early because I need to talk to you, if you have a minute."

"Sure, have a seat. Is everything okay?"

"Everything's fine," she lied. "I'm here to ask a favor. I need to take off Friday. I have some important business that's come up. I hate to ask you, but I really need to take care of this and I can't do it on the weekend.

"I'm sorry to do this on such short notice, but I don't have much choice. If another day would be better, I can put it off, but I'd really like to get it done as soon as possible. If there's any way I can make it up, I'll be happy to do that."

Mercy hesitated. She could rearrange the classes to accommodate Zoe's absence. What bothered her was the fact that Zoe had been on the job such a short time. The idea of an employee requesting a day off when she had been on the job less than a month did not bode well for future dependability. Ian had assured her that Zoe was responsible, even dedicated to her teaching.

The woman sitting across from her appeared to be calm and composed, except for her uncharacteristic rambling. It was enough to make Mercy aware of an underlying tension.

"I'll work something out with one of the other teachers. Are you alright, Zoe? Is there anything else I can do to help?"

"No, thanks, Mercy. I appreciate this."

* * *

Periodically throughout the day Zoe's thoughts returned to the conversation in Mercy's office. She had not been as calm as she had hoped. She had been afraid that Mercy would somehow link the fact that Zoe knew Ian with her request for the day off. Afterward, she realized that idea was totally ridiculous. She was just nervous about what she planned.

Thursday evening, as Zoe parked her rental car, it occurred to her that it might be a good idea to practice driving Ian's car. She refused to refer to it as hers.

After retrieving the keys from her apartment, she unlocked the door of the car and slid into the driver's seat. She took a few minutes to adjust the seat and the mirrors and familiarize herself with the the controls on the panel. That was the easy part.

She turned the key in the ignition, put the car in drive and very slowly pulled away from the curb. She drove around the city for half an hour. The car handled much more easily than she had expected, but that did not eliminate her nervousness. What if she had an accident? It was fully insured, but an accident would delay her plans to return the car to Ian.

She told herself that it would be easier on the open road without the traffic. Of course, she would also have to drive in traffic once she reached Atlanta, but she did not allow herself to dwell on that now.

Friday morning, Zoe was awake early. She had a long drive ahead of her. She felt more comfortable about driving Ian's car, but driving around a familiar city was not the same as driving it more than three hundred miles to Ian's office in Atlanta.

She had never driven a car that size and she was again surprised at how easily it handled. It was beautiful and luxurious. It was a great temptation to ignore her pride and accept it. She reminded herself that the upkeep and insurance would be much more expensive than she could afford.

She also thought about the way he had brushed her off. With that in mind, she wanted nothing from him and she knew she would never feel comfortable with it.

# CHAPTER TWENTY-FIVE

Zoe arrived in Atlanta shortly after one o'clock. She had had to detour from the highway twice to find a rest room, and then again when she reached the city. She called Ian's office for directions when she made her last stop, but deliberately avoided leaving her name.

After locating the office building that housed Ian's company, she drove into the parking garage across the street. She was unconcerned with the expense since she would not be the one paying it.

The queasiness in Zoe's stomach returned as she left the parking garage, but this time it was partly due to nerves. Until she entered the building, it had not occurred to her that there might be a security guard to prevent her from simply going up to Ian's office. When she had called for directions, the receptionist had made no mention of it, but that might have simply been an oversight.

She looked across the lobby, relieved to see only an information desk and the elevators. She did not expect her business to take long, but she made one more trip to the ladies' room as a precaution. It also now occurred to her that Ian might not be in his office and she would have to wait. On the other hand, if that was the case, she could simply leave the keys and a note. The more she thought about it, the more she considered that might be the best solution. Now that the moment had arrived, she was not sure she was up to facing him.

During the elevator ride, not only did her courage return, but also her anger. She had no trouble finding the doors marking the entrance to his company. She was greeted by the receptionist as she entered.

"May I help you?"

"Yes, could you direct me to Ian Roberts's office, please?"

"Certainly. Just go down this hall. You'll see the sign on the door."

Zoe started down the hall. She pretended she did not hear the receptionist when she inquired as to whether she had an appointment. Her heart pounded and, for a moment, she expected that someone would come after her. Evidently, the receptionist did not feel it was important enough to stop her at the entrance. Undoubtedly, there would be a secretary to question her when she reached Ian's office.

Just as she suspected, when Zoe entered the door at the end of the hall she was greeted by another young woman. The name plate on her desk identified her as Karla Michaels. Zoe's anger had reached the boiling point and she was not about to let a secretary stand between her and the object of that anger.

"I'm here to see Mr. Roberts. Is he in?"

The woman at the desk consulted her calendar, frowning.

"I'm afraid there's some mistake. Mr. Roberts has no appointments scheduled this afternoon. However, if you'll give me your name, I'll see if he's available."

"That won't be necessary," Zoe said, moving toward the door beyond the secretary's desk.

Karla did not move fast enough to stop Zoe before she burst into Ian's office. She heard the woman's apology to her employer, but there was no stopping her.


At the time Zoe was parking the car, Ian was already on the receiving end of a lecture. Earlier that week Cal had been indicted on a number of charges, including embezzlement of investment funds. Afterward, Ian received another call from Sharmane.

One minute she was blaming him for their problems and the next she was pleading with him to help. When he tried to explain to her that it was out of his hands and Cal's troubles were his own fault, she hung up on him.

On top of that, he now had to deal with his brother, who had entered his office a few minutes earlier, obviously looking for more than a friendly chat. He stood in front of Ian's desk, staring at his older brother.

"What's on your mind, Derek?"

"Your employees, and your lousy disposition."

Receiving no response from his brother, Derek continued.

"Do you have any idea how many people have come to me in the past few weeks, worried because of something you said to them. Convinced they were on the verge of losing their jobs."

"I haven't threatened anyone's job."

"Not in words, but your attitude has the entire office tiptoeing around you."

"Derek, what do you want from me?"

"I want you to stop moping around and do something about your relationship with Zoe."

"There is no relationship with Zoe."

"That's exactly my point. Have you even attempted to talk to her?"

"There's not much point in that. When she left the

police station without even saying good-bye, I got the message loud and clear."

"Ian, you don't know why she left so abruptly. There could be a perfectly good reason for it. I don't know what happened between you on the island and it's none of my business, but you can't just leave the situation hanging. Talk to her."

"What would you have me say to her?" he said, toying with the paperweight, avoiding his brother's probing gaze.

"For starters, you could tell her you're in love with her."

Ian's head shot up. Their gazes locked—Derek unwilling to retract his statement; Ian unwilling to admit the truth, but unable to deny it.

Finally, Ian shook his head and grunted. "Sure. I go to this woman that I held captive for months and expect her to believe that I'm in love with her. I'm lucky she didn't press charges for kidnapping."

"It seems to me, the fact that she never even mentioned to the police that she had been held against her will is a point in your favor."

He sensed that Ian might be weakening and continued to press his point. He was concerned about the effect Ian's unpleasant attitude was having on his employees, but he was more concerned about his brother's feelings. He could only guess at Zoe's feelings, but he was convinced that his brother would never be satisfied until the two of them reached some conclusion concerning the relationship. That would never happen as long as he ignored the issue.

Ian listened, not saying much. He knew in his heart that his brother was right, he owed it to himself to talk to Zoe, to get some answers to the questions floating around in his head.

He was mulling over his brother's suggestion when the subject of their conversation burst into his office. Startled, he abruptly stood up.

"It's okay, Karla," he assured his secretary, recovering

quickly from his initial shock. "You can go back to your desk."

Zoe marched directly to Ian's desk. He took his seat again as she approached him.

She came right to the point. "I want to talk to you," she said.

She turned and looked pointedly at Derek. "Alone."

Derek put up his hands and backed away from the desk. "No problem. I'll talk to you later, Ian. Just keep in mind what we discussed."

Neither Ian nor Zoe saw the grin on Derek's face as he left the room. The anger emanating from Zoe was unmistakable. He had no idea what had caused it. As far as he was concerned, the fact that it had brought them face to face was all that mattered at the moment.

Derek quietly closed the door behind him, still grinning. He looked at Karla. Her confusion and questions were apparent. Derek did not think it was his place to offer explanations.

"I think it might be best to hold his calls unless it's extremely important," he hinted to the secretary.

Karla simply nodded. The other woman's anger had been obvious. She was aware of the closeness of the brothers and had no compunction about following Derek's suggestion. More than likely, he had an idea of what was going on between the two people behind the closed door.

Ian could not take his eyes off her. She was beautiful. She was wearing a loose-fitting red knit dress that hid most of her body's curves. It made no difference. He already knew every inch of what lay beneath the fabric.

Derek had barely closed the door behind him when Zoe threw the car keys on the desk. That action gave Ian his first hint at the reason for her visit. The stack of papers that had been delivered with the car followed the keys.

"Here are your keys, the registration, and all of the

other papers that were given to me. Your car is parked in the garage across the street."

"It's not my car, Zoe. These papers say it belongs to you. The title is in your name."

"I don't care what the papers or the title say. It is not my car. I wasn't happy with the fact that you paid my rent for six months. I accepted that because, as you so aptly pointed out, I probably would have been evicted otherwise. Although three months rent would have been sufficient for that.

"I even swallowed my pride when I found out you were responsible for my new job because I enjoy it and I honestly feel I can do a lot of good at the center. That doesn't erase the fact that you had no business interfering. I don't need your pity. I can survive on my own."

"I wasn't responsible for your job, Zoe."

"Is Mercy Lincoln a friend of yours?"

"Yes, but that has nothing to do with the issue. How did you get the job?"

"What?"

"How did you get the job? Did Mercy seek you out?"

"No, I answered an ad in the paper. But, do you deny that you talked to her about me?"

Ian did not answer. He knew he could not lie to her.

Zoe's anger escalated. "As you told me when you first questioned me on the island, 'That's not a difficult question.' Did you, or did you not, mention me by name."

Ian sighed. He knew he had no choice but to admit the truth.

"I knew she was looking for a teacher and I mentioned your name. She'd received a few résumés some months ago, but she wasn't satisfied with any of the applicants. I suggested she run the ad again. I admit that I was pretty sure you'd apply for any teaching job that came up.

"Zoe, I know Mercy well enough to know that if she had not been impressed with you, she would never have hired you simply because I mentioned your name. What I did was no more than I would have done for anyone who named me as a reference."

Zoe wanted to believe him. With what she knew about Mercy, she conceded he was probably right. Reluctantly, she set aside the matter of the rent and the job. She was not willing to ignore the car, however.

"You have an explanation for everything, don't you? You think you can just go through life doing whatever you like, simply because you've decided it's the best way. What's your excuse for the car? Was it a bribe to keep me from filing charges for kidnapping? Or was it payment for services rendered? After all, there weren't any other women available on the island. I was just so convenient."

Her last words conjured up all the hurt she had been feeling since he abandoned her at the police station. Her anger was rapidly deteriorating, being replaced by the pain. The tears were burning the backs of her eyelids. She had to get away from him. Before she could act on that thought, the nausea took hold.

Ian flinched in response to her accusation, especially her final statement. She broke off her verbal attack, but before he could utter a word in his defense, she spoke.

"Where's a rest room?"

Ian was taken by surprise at her abrupt change. "I beg your pardon?"

"A rest room."

Ian gestured toward the alcove to his left. "Through there. The door on the right."

Zoe hurried away to the area he indicated. Ian rose from his desk and had only taken a few steps in that direction when he heard her. She had, evidently, worked herself into such an emotional state that she had made herself physically ill.

He could hardly believe this was all because he had bought her a car. The look on her face when she suddenly ended her tirade had given him his first clue that there was more involved than anger. Whatever was responsible, he planned to get to the bottom of it before she left.

A few minutes later, Zoe exited the rest room. She avoided looking in his direction and started toward the door. The nausea had subsided, for the moment. She had finished what she came to do. Now she had to get away from him before the nausea returned. She was halfway to the door when he blocked her path.

Zoe looked up at him, but quickly looked away again. She took a step to the left, attempting to go around him. Ian raised his hands, gently squeezing her shoulders.

"Are you okay?"

"I-I'll be fine."

Ian was not so sure of that. Her color was definitely not normal and she looked as if she might have to make a return trip to the rest room at any second. In spite of her obvious distress, or maybe because of it, he was determined to clear the air between them.

"We have to talk, Zoe."

She shook her head slightly. Ian would not be denied and the anger that had sustained her until now had dissipated. She was too exhausted to resist when he led her to the sofa. After seating her he went to a cabinet across the room and returned with a glass of water. He held it out to her. Zoe accepted it gratefully.

Ian sat down beside her and waited until she had taken a few sips and set the glass on the table. Her hands trembled as he took them in his. She looked down at them, still unable to meet his gaze.

"First of all, Zoe, I admit that you would be well within your rights to file kidnapping charges against me. I did what I could to try to put your life back in order. Believe me, my actions were not motivated by pity; guilt, maybe, but not pity.

"As for your other accusation, I can't believe you would think that. How could you think you meant nothing more than a convenience? What happened between us was beautiful."

There was no response from Zoe, and Ian was beginning to feel that he was fighting a losing battle. It was time to lay all his cards on the table.

"Zoe," he murmured, lifting her chin, "I would never, knowingly, do anything to hurt you. You have to believe that. I love you."

Zoe shook her head, snatching her hands from his grasp. The anger resurfaced.

"You expect me to believe that? You couldn't get rid of me fast enough. What did you do? Ask your friend, Sgt. Travers, to get one of his men to take me off your hands?"

"I couldn't get rid of you? I finished giving my statement to find that you had been in such a hurry to get away that you forgot your suitcase."

"That's not true. After I gave my statement, Officer Miller offered to take me home. I assumed he had his orders from Sgt. Travers."

She shrugged. "I didn't see you anywhere around. I didn't know what else to think except that you were avoiding me, that you didn't want to tell me face to face that you didn't want to see me again."

"Officer Miller may have received his instructions from Travers, but it had nothing to do with me. All I was told was that one of the officers had taken you home."

Ian took her in his arms, pulling her close. "It seems that all this misery was caused by a misunderstanding. I should have come after you that day."

Zoe wanted nothing more than to believe him. "Why didn't you? Come after me, I mean."

"A number of reasons. I guess mostly because I was afraid you would think I was trying to force my attentions on you. The truth is, I began to think that, maybe, you had even felt forced into letting me make love to you when we were on the island. After all, you were there against your will. You might have felt that you had no choice."

Zoe sighed. Even if she were still angry with him, she could not allow him to believe his last statement.

"Ian, I never felt intimidated by you. It was strange, but I was never afraid of you."

"Not then, anyway. The fear came later."

"Don't go there, Ian. We've already discussed the reasons for that confusion and we both agreed that it was settled."

"You're right."

"One more thing. You didn't make love to me on the island. *We* made love. There's a big difference."

He leaned back and looked in her eyes, searching for an answer to his declaration of love. Her eyes seemed to tell him what he longed to hear, but she had not said the words. The situation called for a little persuasion.

He lowered his head slowly, stopping a fraction of any inch before their lips touched. Zoe's eyes closed in anticipation. All the love she had tried to deny rose up in defiance, like a living thing that was determined to be acknowledged.

Ian's lips slowly settled softly on hers, barely touching. His tongue lightly teased the corners of her mouth while his arms tightened around her. Zoe raised her arms, encircling his neck to pull him closer. She wanted more.

Ian was more than willing to give her all she wanted. He opened his mouth to her questing tongue, as he eased her gently back against the sofa pillows. His hand moved to cover her breast, the nipple hardening immediately at his touch.

When he first heard it, Ian mistook her empty stomach's protest for a moan of passion. A moment later he realized the truth. Zoe's eyes popped open in surprise and embarrassment as she abruptly broke the kiss. Ian shook his head, grinning as he sat up. Zoe avoided his gaze as she smoothed the wrinkles from her dress.

"In the future, I'll have to remember to feed you before I decide to get romantic. I assume you haven't had lunch?"

Zoe cleared her throat. "No, I haven't."

He stood up and started walking toward the door. "I'll take care of that. What would you like?"

"I don't know. A sandwich, I guess."

"A hamburger?"

Zoe thought about the fragile stability of her stomach. "No, I think something lighter."

"How about chicken salad? The deli downstairs has great chicken salad."

"That's fine."

Still grinning, Ian went to the door. As frustrated as he was, the joy that welled up in him far outweighed any momentary disappointment. He realized that it was probably just as well that her stomach grumbling had interrupted them. Otherwise, it was quite possible that before long they would both have been lying naked on the sofa.

Zoe took a deep breath in an attempt to recover some semblance of composure. One little kiss and the passion that had become a pleasant memory had returned in full force.

# CHAPTER
# TWENTY-SIX

Karla was even more confused than she had been at Zoe's arrival when Ian exited his office, grinning. He pulled out his wallet and handed her a bill.

"My guest hasn't had lunch, Karla. Would you go down and get her a sandwich from the deli, please. Chicken salad will be fine."

Karla took the money. She had a million questions, but held her tongue. It was none of her business.

"Sure, Ian. Anything else?"

"No, thanks. The sandwich will be enough."

Ian reentered his office a few minutes later to find Zoe standing at the window. She turned toward him, her composure intact. Between the anger, the emotional pain, and the passion, she was calm for the first time since walking through the door.

"That was quick," she said. Then she noticed his empty hands.

"I sent Karla downstairs to the deli. She shouldn't be long. Meanwhile, would you like something to drink?" he asked, on his way to the cabinet across the room.

"There's orange juice, cranberry juice, milk, assorted soft drinks. There's even wine, if you'd like something stronger."

"Orange juice is fine."

He had just placed the glass on the table when the telephone rang. He went to answer it and Zoe went to get her drink. She watched him, his earlier declaration of love running through her mind. She couldn't believe it. He loved her! How could he love her? He barely knew her.

*You're in love with him, Zoe. Why is it easier to believe that you could fall in love with him in a few short months? You questioned your own feelings, too, remember. But, you no longer have any doubt about them.*

She could not take her eyes off him. She wanted nothing more than to be with him, to make a life together, to have his children. His children! She had to tell him about the baby.

How could she explain that she had lied when she told him there was no chance that she was pregnant? What if he refused to believe it was his child? What if he turned her away?

She had promised herself she would ask for nothing from him. What if he thought she was after money? The nausea returned. She hurried to the bathroom.

Ian's attention was drawn to her as she practically ran toward the alcove. Something was wrong. The first time he had assumed that it was nerves and emotional upset that had made her ill. Now he was concerned that it was more than that.

His thoughts were interrupted by a knock on the office door. He went to answer it just as Zoe returned from the bathroom and walked back to the sofa.

"Thanks, Karla," he said, taking the container from his secretary.

The nausea had subsided once again. Zoe hoped she would be able to keep down the sandwich Ian had ordered. She also hoped he did not ask too many questions about her illness. She was still trying to come up with the right words to tell him about the baby. That problem was uppermost in her mind when Ian sat down beside her, placing the container on the table.

"Here's your sandwich. Are you sure you'll be able to keep it down? It appears you may have picked up a stomach virus."

"You may be right. I'm so hungry, though, that I have to give it a try."

"Would you like some more orange juice? Or maybe some ginger ale would be better?"

"I think you're right. I'll try the ginger ale."

After he set the glass of ginger ale on the table, he went back to his desk. Zoe breathed a sigh of relief that he did not sit down beside her. She was not sure she could have eaten a bite with him sitting there watching her.

Ian watched her as he picked up the telephone. He made several business calls, but his eyes never left her the whole time. She ate slowly, but at least it seemed that her stomach problems had subsided.

For the first time since she entered the office Zoe had time to examine her surroundings. The focal point of the room was the oversized mahogany desk where he was now seated. It was a strikingly beautiful piece of furniture with four inches of ornate carving around the entire perimeter just below the surface. It was certainly not what one would normally expect to find in a business office, but oddly enough, it did not seem out of place.

The desk was situated in front of a wall comprised totally of windows that overlooked downtown Atlanta. Against the wall to Ian's right was a matching mahogany credenza that looked to be at least six feet long. Its doors and the mirror hanging on the wall above it were framed in the same carved pattern found on the desk.

A lamp with a tall, urn-shaped, mottled gold-and-brown base was reflected in the mirror. A carved ebony statue of an African warrior, a large shallow wooden bowl, and a stack of small grass baskets completed the arrangement on top of the credenza. On the floor to the side was a tall vase containing a cluster of large dieffenbachia leaves.

At the moment, she was seated on an overstuffed burgundy, green, and beige print sofa flanked by hunter green armchairs. A large square coffee table completed the informal conversation area.

In a separate corner to his left was an armoire, identical in style to the desk and credenza. Its doors stood open, revealing a computer and the other tools of his trade. Underfoot, a lush beige carpet offset the dark furniture and pale gold textured walls. The overall decor was luxurious, but still managed to give a feeling of comfort.

During these observations, Zoe had finished her sandwich. She was grateful that the queasiness was gone, at least for the time being. The chips and pickle went untouched. She did not want to push her luck. She was just beginning to relax, thinking she could go back home and have a little more time to collect her thoughts, when Ian rose from his desk and walked over to her. She realized a quick escape was out of the question when he sat down next to her.

"Now that I don't have to worry about you fainting from hunger, we need to talk. I won't suggest that we take up where we left off. I think we both know where that would take us and we need to have a talk first.

"You look a little better now that you've eaten. How do you feel?"

"Much better. Maybe I was just hungry and upset," she suggested, avoiding his eyes.

Ian was aware that she had yet to make any mention of her own feelings. Maybe the love he had expressed was one-sided. It was hard to believe that she did not feel the same about him, but that might only be wishful thinking.

"Zoe, do you have any idea how glad I was to see you walk through that door? I've missed you. I've been miserable, but I couldn't do anything about it because I was afraid to come to you. I was convinced that you wanted nothing more to do with me. Derek accused me of alienating most of my staff with my grouchiness."

"I wouldn't have come if it hadn't been for the car. I'm still not comfortable with it. I understand that you felt the need to replace mine, since it was stolen while I was on the island."

"Then, what's the problem?"

"You really don't get it, do you?"

Zoe paused and shook her head. She looked up at him. His puzzled expression made her realize that he really did not understand.

"Ian, if you had bought a nice midsize used car it would have been a reasonable replacement for the one that was stolen and destroyed. That brand new luxury car parked in the garage across the street is hardly on the same level as the one I lost."

"I wanted to be sure that you had one that was dependable. A used car can be a real headache. Even a new one, depending on the make, can be a lemon. I know that you have that possibility with any car, but it's less likely with a more expensive one."

"I can't keep that car. Aside from the fact that I'd have to come up with a good story to tell my family, my own conscience won't let me accept something that expensive."

"There is a way to get around that."

He hesitated. He had already played most of his cards. He knew what he wanted. It only remained to find out what she felt.

"What's your solution?"

"Consider it a wedding gift. Even your family couldn't object to your fiancé giving you a car."

Zoe's mouth dropped open. When she found her voice it was barely audible.

"What are you saying?"

"I'm asking you to marry me. I love you, Zoe. I don't intend to let you walk out of my life again."

"Ian, you've only known me a few months. You know hardly anything about me. You don't even know how old I am."

"You're right, but it doesn't matter. I know you're over twenty-one because you told me you had been teaching for a while before going to work for Burnett.

"Anything else we have a lifetime to discover."

She could not look him in the eye. All her dreams were coming true. He loved her. He wanted to marry her. And she would destroy it all when she told him she had lied about the pregnancy.

"What is it, sweetheart? What's the real problem? I have the feeling that our short acquaintance is not the only reason for your hesitation."

He reached over and lifted her chin, forcing her eyes to meet his. Zoe's dilemma showed on her face.

"Zoe? Do you love me? It's alright to tell me the truth. I need to know."

Tears came to her eyes. She tried to turn away, but he refused to allow it. She could lie again. She could tell him what she felt was only a physical attraction. Looking in those ebony eyes, she knew lying was not an option.

"I do love you, Ian, but I can't marry you. There's something I have to tell you. You'll probably change your mind when you hear it."

"Nothing will make me change my mind, Zoe. I love you. I told you I have no intention of letting you walk away from me again."

Zoe took a deep breath and closed her eyes.

"I'm pregnant."

Ian struggled with the thoughts and emotions that rushed through him. Pregnant! She was carrying his child. How could he have been so blind? He should have guessed. The persistent nausea and the loose-fitting dress were obvious clues. Then he recalled their last few days on the island.

"How could that be, Zoe? You supposedly were suffering

from your period when we were on the island. Why did
you lie?"

Zoe felt a small sense of relief. At least he had not raised
the question of the child not being his.

"I couldn't let myself get close to you after I saw you
with Chad. I never dreamed my excuse would come back
to haunt me."

There was no way she could deny his right to be angry.
All things considered, he was actually rather calm, but she
detected an edge to his voice when he responded.

"If you hadn't come here to return the car, exactly when
were you planning to tell me? Or were you ever planning
to tell me."

"Of course I was planning to tell you, after the child
was born. I would never keep you from your child or deny
him his father. The only reason I didn't come to you
sooner was because I thought you wanted to break off the
relationship and I didn't want you to think . . ."

She stopped. She did not want to raise the issue of
money. Evidently that had not occurred to him and she
decided to leave well enough alone.

"What didn't you want me to think?"

Zoe sighed. "I didn't want you to think I was coming to
you for money."

Ian shook his head. He took her in his arms.

"Oh, Zoe. How could you think I'd ever believe that. I
almost had to force you to take the clothes I bought for
you. Besides, I remember expressly telling you that if there
were any unexpected consequences of our lovemaking I
would be here for you. You were the one who was so sure
it wouldn't happen from just one time."

He leaned back and wiped the tears that she had been
unable to hold back. She was so lovely, even with a tear-
streaked face. She also looked so vulnerable. Why hadn't
he noticed it before? He should have seen it, even through
the angry tirade.

"So, what date shall we set for the wedding?"

Zoe opened her mouth to remind him that she had not accepted his proposal. Ian forestalled her, the look in her eyes telling him what was on her mind.

"Zoe, I hope you're not planning to refuse. I love you. You've admitted you love me. Your carrying my child. What possible reason could you have for refusing?"

"There's still the fact that we've only known each other a few short months. What will your family think?"

Ian grinned. "Just before you arrived, Derek was chewing me out for letting you get away."

"You told Derek about us?"

"I didn't need to. He guessed that my lousy disposition was related to the fact that you had disappeared from my life. So, stop trying to change the subject. Will you marry me, Zoe?"

"I've been miserable, too, Ian. I do love you. More than I thought possible, even if I had known you for years. I suppose no matter how long you know someone, there aren't any guarantees when it comes to marriage. I guess you just have to take some things on faith."

"So?"

"Yes, Ian, I'll marry you. I don't know how I thought I could come here and see you and walk away."

Ian heaved an exaggerated sigh. "Do you have any idea how exhausting this has been? Please tell me you won't make me work this hard ever again."

Zoe smiled. "I can only promise you won't have to work this hard emotionally. As for the physical work, that's up to you."

"If you're referring to what I think you're referring to, that, sweetheart, is not work. It's pleasure."

He was still holding her and his arms tightened, pulling her closer. His lips came down on hers as his hands slowly eased down the zipper of her dress. With little maneuvering, she was soon lying on top of him, every stitch of her clothes in a heap on the floor beside the sofa.

Before long they were lost in their own world, reigniting

the passion they had discovered on a small island a short time ago. Ian's last coherent thought before ecstasy claimed him was appreciation for the lock on his office door and gratitude that he had remembered to put it to use.

can readers has had di:..e.red on . such bread a...
of the app... lett r, but conform... though... before we thi...
channel has wed ...pre. inter for the loc... on his table
chair and pointing that both ... announce... to put it to
one.

# EPILOGUE

"Savannah, honey, don't swing your basket around like that," Zoe warned her young daughter. "You'll make all the petals fall out and then you won't have any to sprinkle when you walk down the aisle."

The child obeyed, for all of two minutes. Zoe watched her out of the corner of her eye. She shook her head. It was nothing new. Her daughter came by her willfulness honestly. All told, the little girl had probably spent about a year of her young life in "time out."

She was a beautiful and, usually, a very sweet child. She had her father's ebony eyes and bronze complexion, but she had her mother's smile. She also had the long, thick hair Zoe remembered from her own childhood.

At the moment, it was arranged in two clusters of curls on either side of her head. Dark green velvet ribbons and white rosebuds offset the dark curls. The green velvet skirt of her dress matched the ribbons and the white lace bodice was trimmed in the green velvet.

When the basket started swinging again, as Zoe had expected, she decided it was time for action. Without a word, she walked over to the child and held out her hand. Savannah was intent on her mischief and did not see her mother approaching. She looked up now and pouted.

"You might as well put the lip in, Savannah. You may have the basket when it's time for you to walk down the aisle. Why don't you sit down and look at your book?"

The child knew when she was beaten. She handed the basket over and went to sit in the rocker on the other side of her parents' bedroom. Zoe placed the basket of rose petals on the dresser just as her sister entered the room.

"Blake's dressed and the limo just arrived," Cleo announced.

"Let me help you with that," she offered, seeing her sister's attempts to attach the train to her wedding gown.

The gown was an ivory sheath with beaded lace sleeves and a bodice that ended in a vee just below the waist. The satin skirt was bordered in the same beaded lace at the hem. The slit in the back of the skirt was hidden by a detachable train.

The wide, low-cut neckline bared her shoulders. Zoe had hesitated to buy the gown because of the cleavage exposed by the low-cut neckline. Cleo had talked her into it, insisting that it was perfectly decent.

Zoe had decided to forego a traditional headpiece. Instead, the loose curls atop her head were intertwined with white rosebuds, orange blossoms, and glossy magnolia leaves. A cloud of tulle was clipped high on the back of her head, just beneath the cluster of loose curls.

After Cleo attached the train, Zoe clipped on the pearl and diamond drop earrings that matched the pendant nestled between her breasts. She glanced over at her daughter and took one last look in the mirror. Surprisingly, Savannah was still occupied with her book.

"Alright, Savannah," she said, slipping on the ivory satin pumps. "It's time to go."

* * *

A few minutes later, Zoe and the remainder of the wedding party were on their way to the church. The ceremony to renew their vows had been Ian's idea. They had been married five years ago in a very simple ceremony in Zoe's parents' home. She had not felt comfortable with the idea of walking down the aisle for an elaborate church wedding since by then she was five months pregnant with her daughter.

When they had attended Zoe's brother's wedding, Cleo had mentioned to Ian that Zoe had always wanted a big wedding. At that time, she was eight months pregnant with their second child, Blake. When their son was born, Ian presented her with his certificate "Good for One Elaborate Wedding, With All the Trimmings."

She was unsure that idea was any better than having a large wedding in the beginning. She finally agreed, rationalizing that it would be more of a celebration to share with their families and friends.

She did not know that Ian's suggestion was as much for his own benefit as it was for her. After watching Alexander's bride-to-be walk down the aisle, he could not erase the picture from his mind.

Of course, in Ian's fantasy, the radiant woman in the beautiful gown was his wife. He wanted to make that fantasy a reality for both of them.

He had been considering the idea of renewing their vows even before she became pregnant with their son. They had married rather hastily and had known each other such a short time before that.

He hoped that she had no doubts about his love, but it would be good to say the words to each other again.

* * *

They arrived at the church fifteen minutes before the ceremony was to begin. Cleo had suggested that they should arrive earlier, but Zoe insisted she did not want to be standing around waiting. She told herself she was being ridiculous. Why should she be so nervous? She was already married to the man waiting inside the church.

"Where's Daddy?" Savannah asked as they climbed the stairs. "Grandma said he'd be here."

"We'll see him in a little while, sweetheart."

There was a flurry of activity when they entered the church. Savannah had caught a glimpse of her father standing near the altar and had to be physically restrained.

Within minutes, the lights had been dimmed and the church was alight with dozens of candles. The wedding party lined up. The bridesmaids wore gowns of deep green velvet. Each of them carried a bouquet of white roses, baby's breath, and magnolia leaves with a candle in the center of the arrangement. Their headpieces were crowns of the same white roses, baby's breath, and shiny magnolia leaves. Each escort carried his own taper in his free hand.

Zoe had seen her daughter's disappointment at the rehearsal when she was informed that she would not be carrying a candle. She patiently explained that Savannah could not carry a candle since she needed both hands free to perform her important duty. The child had looked at the basket and pondered that explanation with a frown. She had finally conceded that her mother was right.

The little whirlwind had calmed down when her turn came to walk down the aisle. By then, she was so intent upon her task of scattering rose petals that she was halfway down the aisle before she started getting nervous. She looked up at a beaming Ian who winked and nodded his encouragement. When she reached the altar, she detoured before taking her place on the side.

Marching straight over to her father, she whispered loudly, "Did I do good, Daddy?"

Ian smiled. "You were perfect, angel."

Satisfied, she skipped to the other side of the altar and took her place next to her Aunt Cleo. Ian's attention was drawn away from his daughter when the congregation stood up, signaling Zoe's approach.

Ian caught his breath as she appeared in the doorway to begin her march. His wife. His beautiful, extraordinary wife. She had always filled him with an amazing sense of joy and contentment. Watching her now, he was filled with another emotion—gratitude.

Standing beside Ian, Derek saw the look on his brother's face and grinned. Having watched their relationship develop, he had never had any doubt of the deep love they had for each other.

He had assured her sister of this when she candidly expressed doubts about their marriage after such a brief acquaintance. He glanced past the altar at Cleo and winked. She smiled back and gave a slight nod in agreement.

Zoe took a deep breath and clutched her father's arm. She could not believe she was still nervous. After living with Ian for five years, she had no doubt of his love, or his commitment. Her mother and Cleo had assured her that her jitters were a normal reaction after the months of preparation.

She had a moment of apprehension as she watched her daughter make a detour before taking her proper place beside Cleo. As Zoe began her march, she glanced down the long aisle and her gaze locked with her husband's. Even from that distance, the obvious love in his eyes dispelled any remaining tension.

When she reached the altar she handed her bouquet to Cleo and turned her attention to Ian. He smiled, enfolding her hand in his as her father took his seat. From that moment, her gaze never left Ian's as they repeated the vows they had taken five years earlier. They had briefly considered writing their own vows for this ceremony. When they recalled the words they had spoken at their wedding, they decided that nothing they could write themselves could be any more beautiful than the age-old vows.

Zoe had been preoccupied when her father performed his part in the ceremony, but her full attention was now on the promises that were being uttered by Ian. Their attention never wavered from each other as they each, in turn, repeated the vows to love, honor, and cherish.

Zoe was wrapped up in the cloak of love that had been woven around them. The brief kiss they shared at the end was simply not enough to express the emotions that filled every ounce of her being. Ian smiled at the frustration that showed on her face.

"Don't look so disappointed, baby," he murmured for her ears only. "I promise to make it up to you later."

Zoe smiled back at him. "I won't forget that. I plan to hold you to that promise, sweetheart."

Ian tucked her arm in his and chuckled. The organist struck the first chord, and he urged her down the aisle to await the hugs and kisses and expressions of love from their families and friends.

Some time later, the couple entered the reception hall. They were greeted by the cheers of the friends and family already assembled.

"I keep thinking I should send a thank-you note to Burnett," he murmured, enfolding her in his arms.

"Why on earth would you do that?" she asked, frowning.

"Look at it this way. If it hadn't been for him, we might never have met."

Just then the band started playing "Always and Forever." Zoe looked up at Ian and felt her eyes misting over.

"Somehow, I think we would have met, with or without Burnett," she whispered.

"You're probably right. We were meant to be together, sweetheart," he murmured, gently kissing away the tears that had begun rolling down her cheeks.

As if to punctuate his statement, he lowered his head, his lips capturing hers in a long, lingering kiss. The kiss they shared on the dance floor was nothing like the brief meeting of lips that had taken place in church.

The vows they had exchanged earlier proclaimed the promises of enduring love and devotion. This kiss was a promise of the continuing passion that had never diminished since that brief interlude on the island.

*Dear Readers,*

*I hope you enjoyed this novel, which was a slight departure from my other two novels. The problems of Ian and Zoe involved more than the usual ones of any relationship.*

*I have to explain that, although there is probably an island that could fit the description, Blake's Island is a figment of my imagination. The idea of an interlude on a deserted island was simply too romantic to ignore.*

*Please write and let me know what you thought of this story. I enjoy hearing from you.*

*Sincerely,*

*Marilyn Tyner*
*P.O. Box 219*
*Yardley, PA 19067*
*email:mtyner1@juno.com*

# Coming Soon from Arabesque Books . . .

**___ONE LOVE by Lynn Emery**
1-58314-046-8                                    $4.99US/$6.50CAN
When recovering alcoholic Lanessa Thomas is thrown back with Alexander St. Romain—the only man she ever loved and the one she hurt the most—they must battle bitter distrust and pain to save their second chance at love.

**___DESTINED by Adrienne Ellis Reeves**
1-58314-047-6                                    $4.99US/$6.50CAN
When Leah Givens eloped as a teen, her father forced her to leave her new husband immediately. But now, thirteen years later, her one and only is back. Now, they must decide if they are strong enough to heal the scars from years of separation and build a love that is destined.

**___IMPETUOUS by Dianne Mayhew**
1-58314-043-3                                    $4.99US/$6.50CAN
Liberty Sutton made the worst mistake of her life when she gave sole custody of her baby to its father. But when she meets executive Jarrett Irving, and is unexpectedly given a chance to reclaim a life with her child, she must reconcile her troubled past with a future that promises happiness.

**___UNDER A BLUE MOON by Shirley Harrison**
1-58314-049-2                                    $4.99US/$6.50CAN
Knocked unconscious and left to die, Angie Manchester awakens on an exotic island with handsome Dr. Matthew Sinclair at her side—and no memory of her identity. Thrown together by chance and danger, but drawn by overwhelming desire, the two must take cover in the island's lush forest where they succumb to a passion that comes but once in a lifetime.

---

Call toll free **1-888-345-BOOK** to order by phone or use this coupon to order by mail.
Name _____
Address _____
City _____ State _____ Zip _____
Please send me the books I have checked above.
I am enclosing                                           $ _____
Plus postage and handling*                               $ _____
Sales tax (in NY, TN, and DC)                            $ _____
Total amount enclosed                                    $ _____
*Add $2.50 for the first book and $.50 for each additional book.
Send check or money order (no cash or CODs) to: **Arabesque Books, Dept. C.O. 850 Third Avenue, 16ᵗʰ Floor, New York, NY 10022**
Prices and numbers subject to change without notice.
All orders subject to availabilty.
Visit our website at **www.arabesquebooks.com.**